Billy Stuart
and the Sea of a Thousand Dangers

Book 3

The Zintrepids

Alain M. Bergeron
Illustrated by Sampar

Translated by Sophie B. Watson

ORCA BOOK PUBLISHERS

Text copyright © 2019 Alain M. Bergeron
Illustrations copyright © 2019 Sampar
Originally published in French in 2012 by Éditions Michel Quintin
under the title *Billy Stuart La mer aux mille dangers*
Translation copyright © 2019 Sophie B. Watson

Cataloguing in Publication information available from Library and Archives Canada

Issued in print and electronic formats.
ISBN 9781459823433 (softcover) | ISBN 9781459823440 (PDF) | ISBN 9781459823457 (EPUB)

Library of Congress Control Number: 2019934026
Simultaneously published in Canada and the United States in 2019

Summary: In this illustrated novel for middle-grade readers, Billy Stuart and his loyal Scout
group have inadvertently traveled through time and have to cross an ocean full of danger.

*Orca Book Publishers is committed to reducing the consumption of nonrenewable resources in the
making of our books. We make every effort to use materials that support a sustainable future.*

Orca Book Publishers gratefully acknowledges the support for its publishing programs provided
by the following agencies: the Government of Canada, the Canada Council for the Arts and the
Province of British Columbia through the BC Arts Council and the Book Publishing Tax Credit.

We acknowledge the financial support of the Government of Canada through the National
Translation Program for Book Publishing, an initiative of the *Roadmap for Canada's Official
Languages 2013-2018: Education, Immigration, Communities,* for our translation activities.

Cover and interior illustrations by Sampar
Translated by Sophie B. Watson

ORCA BOOK PUBLISHERS
orcabook.com

Printed and bound in China.

22 21 20 19 • 4 3 2 1

Table of Contents

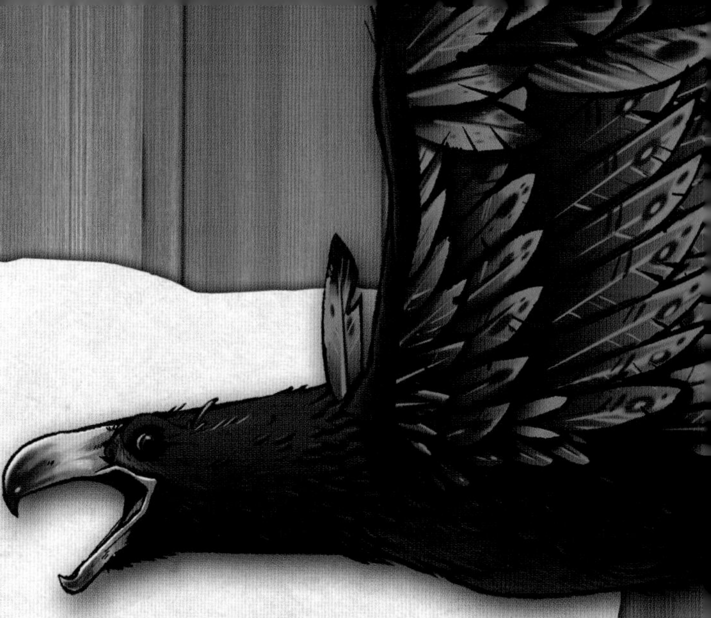

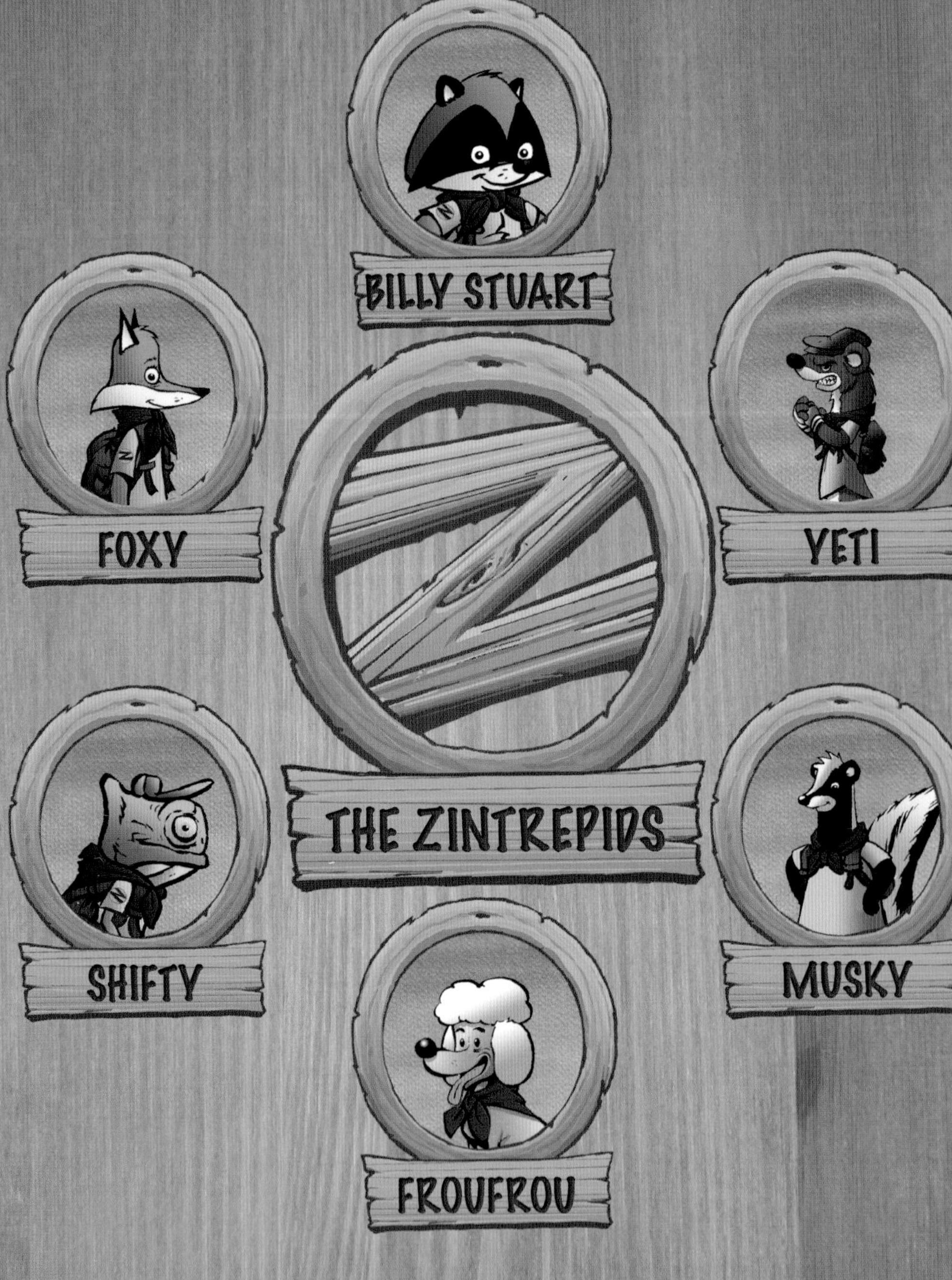
BILLY STUART
FOXY
YETI
THE ZINTREPIDS
SHIFTY
MUSKY
FROUFROU

DEAR READER,

Billy Stuart wasn't exactly elected to this particular position. He doesn't wear a magical ring on his finger like Frodo. He doesn't have a secret collection of masks or stones hidden in his drawers like Zelda. He hasn't walked through life accompanied by a daemon like Lyra. Nor does he have a distinctive lightning-shaped scar on his forehead like Harry. Basically, the future of the world does not rest on his thin and bony shoulders.

Billy Stuart is just a young, ordinary raccoon who has experienced some extraordinary adventures.

Here is the third adventure he told me about.

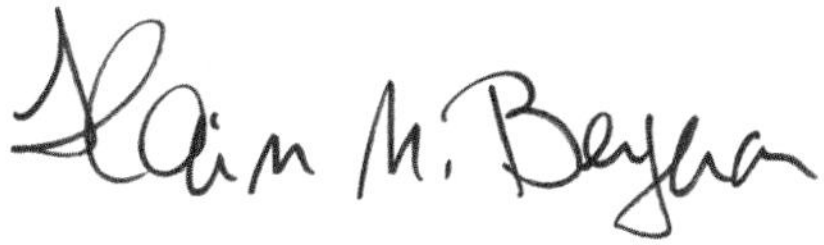

One twenty-second of June, in the town of Cavendish.

Author's note

First of all, let me introduce myself. I am Alain M. Bergeron, the author to whom Billy Stuart has told his many adventures. Over the course of these pages, you will notice I feel the need to add my two cents directly into Billy's story, so as to:

- clarify a point or some bit of information;
- add a personal commentary;
- amuse myself;
- all of the above.

My presence in this book and the following ones will be through the use of an author's note. These little interruptions look like a note glued to a page.

And now, you can get back to your reading.

A.M.B

THE RECAP

Billy Stuart has promised to take care of FrouFrou, the MacTerrings' dog, for the whole summer and is dreading the long days of July and August. Then he gets a letter from his grandfather, Virgil, who claims to have found a cave with a passage that lets him travel in time. Billy Stuart sets out on his grandfather's trail, accompanied by his Scout pack, the Zintrepids—and FrouFrou. What Billy doesn't know is that once they go down the fateful path his grandfather took, there will be no turning back.

Billy and his friends become trapped in another world and another time, ending up as prisoners in the Minotaur's lair.

After escaping the terrible Minotaur's clutches and miraculously finding their way out of the labyrinth, Billy and his friends board a ship that sails directly into a storm on the sea of a thousand dangers. A storm that threatens their lives...

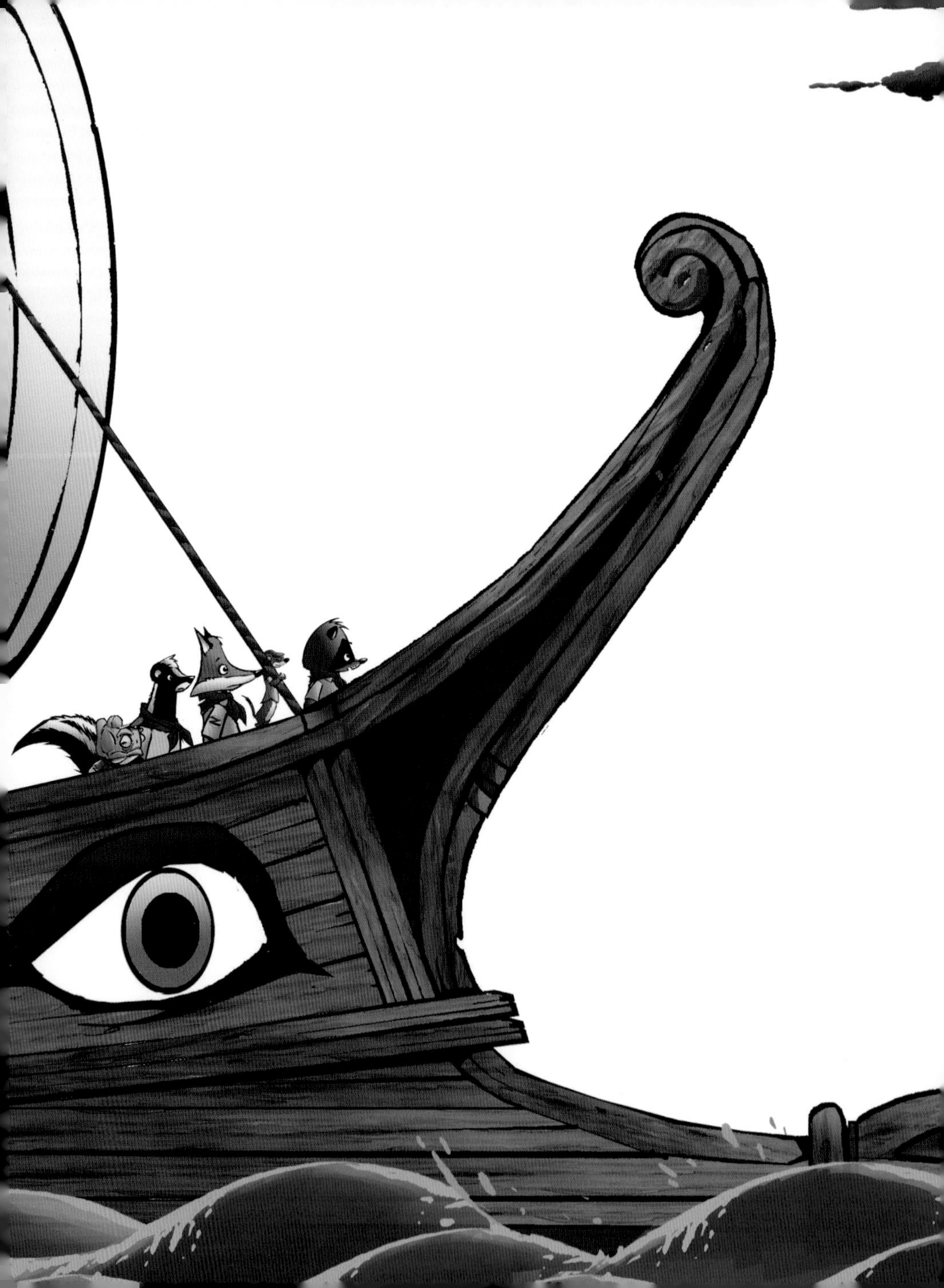

The Storm

That would be too ridiculous!

It would be too ridiculous if a storm ended our adventurers'
lives after they've surmounted all those other obstacles!

Leaning on the gunwale, we watch the spectacle unfolding in the distance. An enormous mass of clouds, DARK and MENACING, is throwing lightning bolts into the sea. The sound of thunder bounces off the waves, shaking us to the core.

"Is there a way to go around the thunderstorm?" I ask the captain.

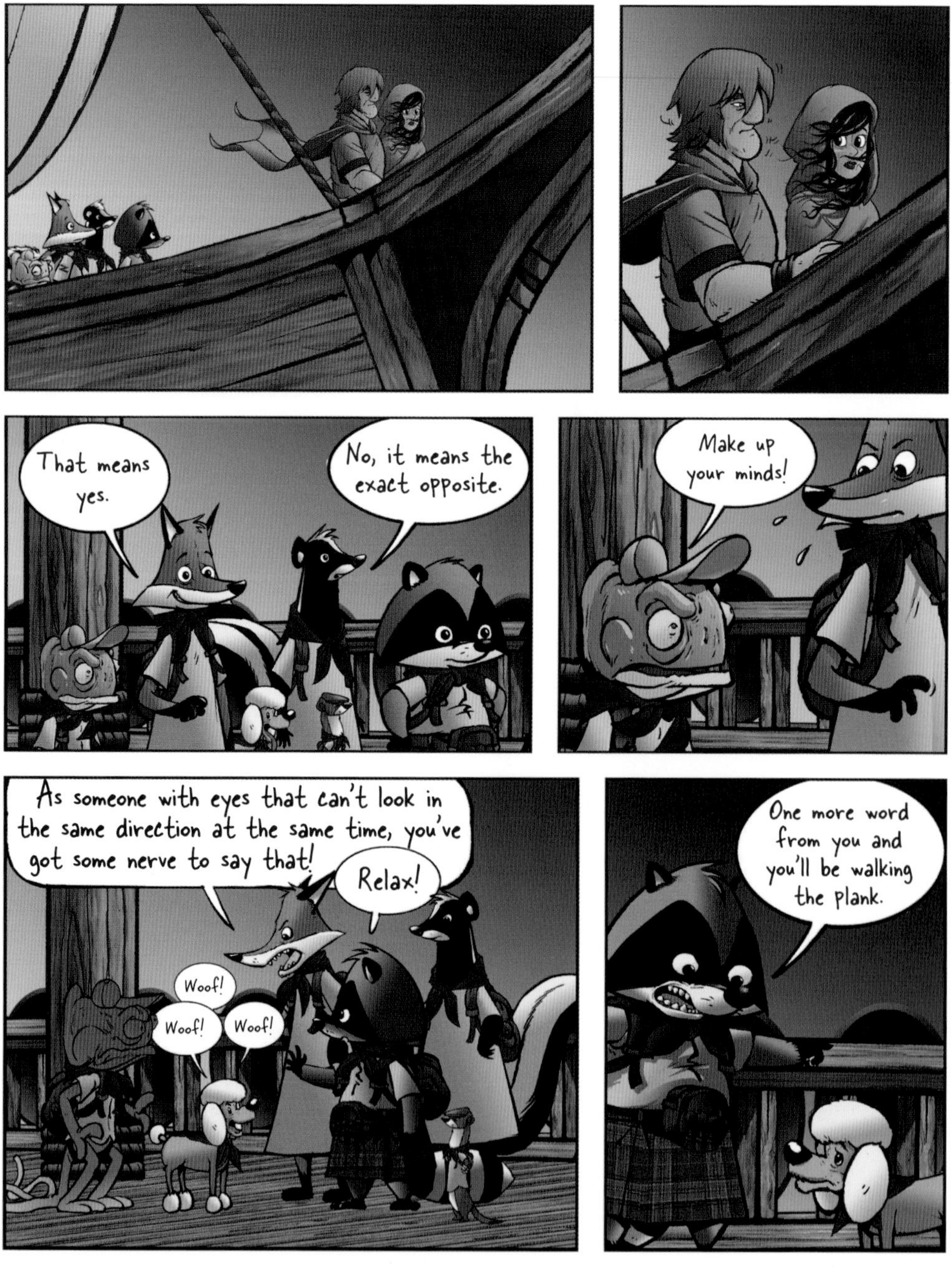
That means yes.
No, it means the exact opposite.
Make up your minds!
As someone with eyes that can't look in the same direction at the same time, you've got some nerve to say that!
Relax!
Woof!
Woof!
Woof!
One more word from you and you'll be walking the plank.

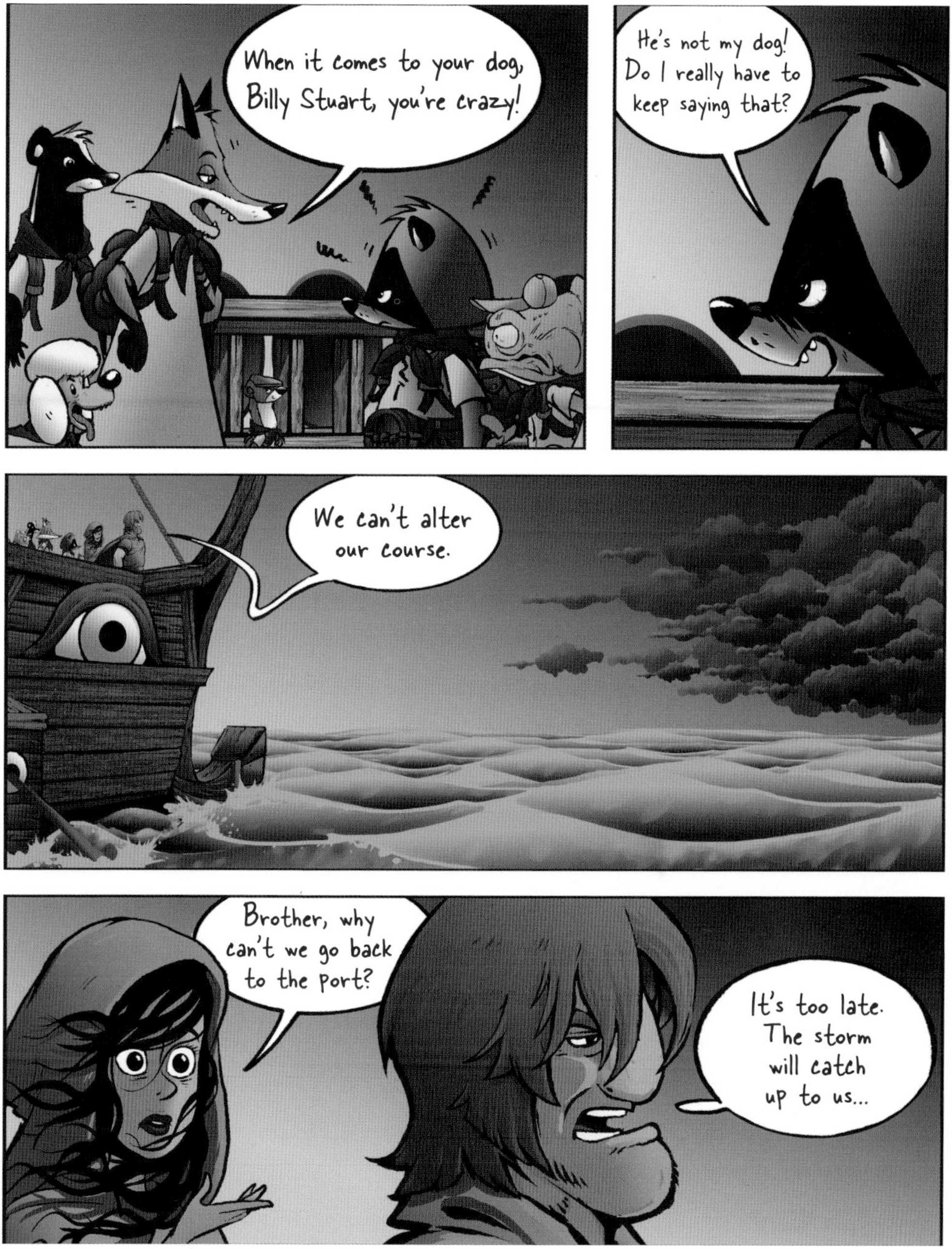
When it comes to your dog, Billy Stuart, you're crazy!
He's not my dog! Do I really have to keep saying that?
We can't alter our course.
Brother, why can't we go back to the port?
It's too late. The storm will catch up to us...

Loslobos is right. The **CLOUDS** that an hour ago were far out over the sea have now advanced considerably. They are blocking out the midafternoon sun, and the wind is rising. The gap between the LIGHTNING and the **THUNDER** is getting shorter and shorter.

It's easy to calculate how close lightning is to you. Sound moves at 340 meters per second. Count the number of seconds between seeing the lightning and hearing the thunder and then divide by three. For example, if you count nine seconds before you hear the thunder after the lightning, divide nine by three, which gives you three. This tells you that the lightning struck three kilometers away. And yes, it would be a good idea to run for shelter.

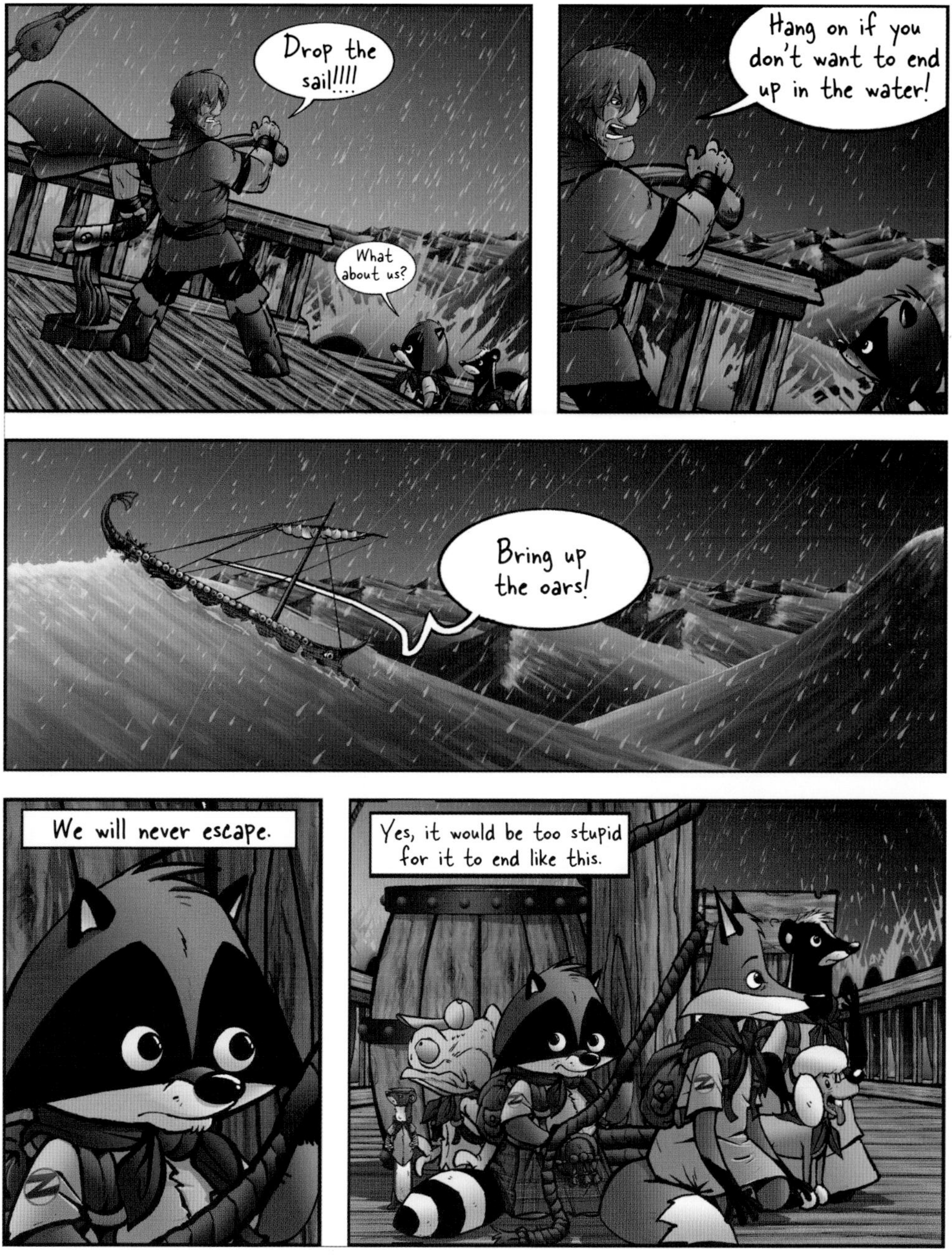

Drop the sail!!!!!
What about us?
Hang on if you don't want to end up in the water!
Bring up the oars!
We will never escape.
Yes, it would be too stupid for it to end like this.

FUNNY FACES!

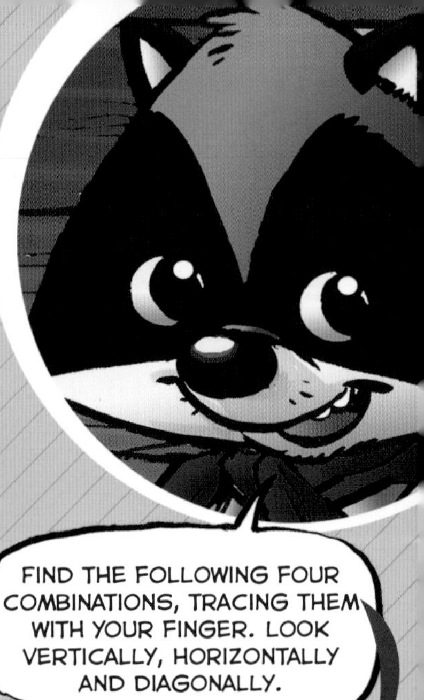
FIND THE FOLLOWING FOUR COMBINATIONS, TRACING THEM WITH YOUR FINGER. LOOK VERTICALLY, HORIZONTALLY AND DIAGONALLY.

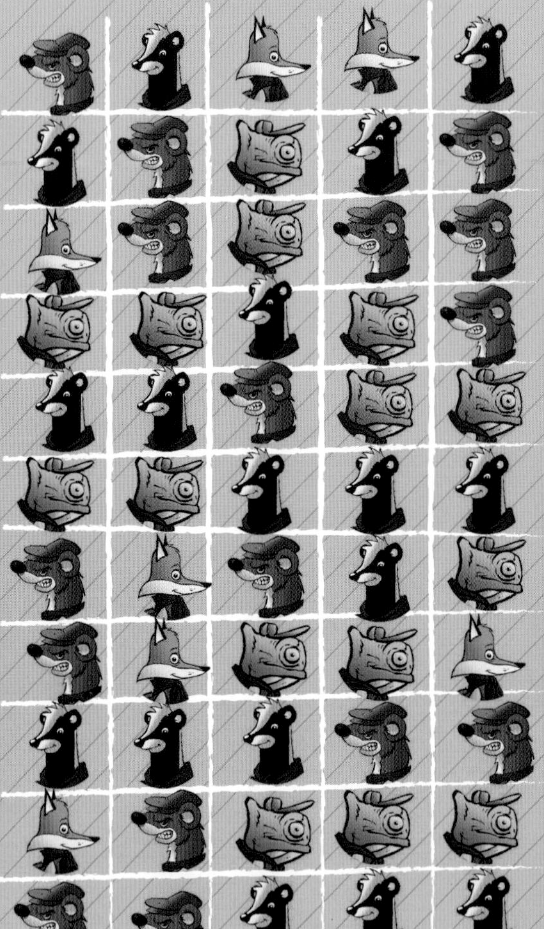

1 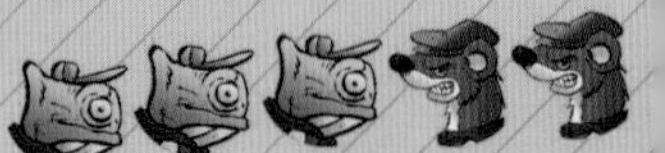

2 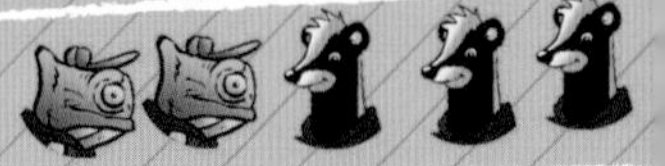

3 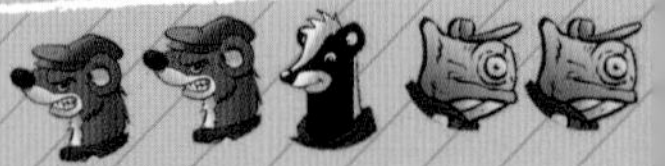

4 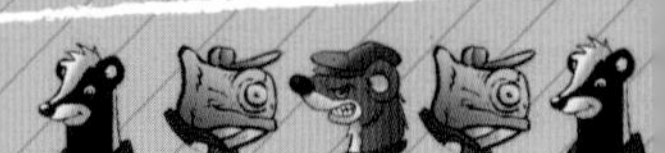

BE CAREFUL—
DON'T LOOSE
YOUR HEAD!

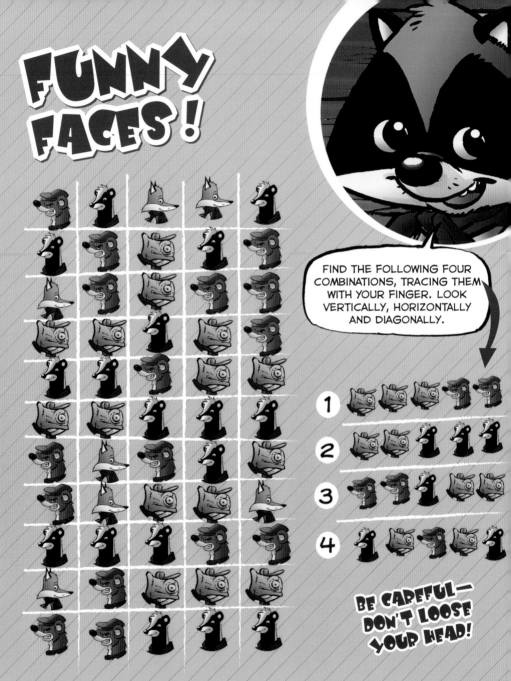

Solution on page 142.

Chapter 2

Astrophobia

As the storm gets closer and closer, I get more and more nervous. If I could, I would hide under a chair in the captain's cabin. I would stuff broccoli in my ears to drown out the deafening thunder. That's all broccoli is good for anyway! YUCK!

My mother forces me to eat it—only now and then, according to her, but way too often in my opinion. She always tells me how good it is for me, even though every time I eat it I turn as green as the broccoli.

Billy Stuart continued talking about broccoli's lack of good qualities. I reminded him that broccoli is the "hero" of the vegetable world because of its nutritional value. A serving of broccoli has twice as many vitamins as an orange. To which Billy said, "Would you drink a glass of broccoli juice to get your day started?" He has a point. That's the end of my author's note, and now we get back to the raging storm.

I realize at this moment that I am super scared. I'm worried about this **STORM** that's **CHARGING** toward us. It reminds me of the one that drove us into Belcher's Cavern.

In keeping with Billy Stuart's usual bad luck, a thunderstorm broke out in the town of Cavendish the last time we met. The thunder's effects on our friend are clearly visible. He shakes. He's nervous. At the slightest strike, he tucks in his head, as if that will protect him. Mind you, if anyone understands this, it's me. The day of the storm, we two astrophobes (people who have an exaggerated fear of thunderstorms) continued our interview in a closet.

A thunderclap makes me jump with fright. My teeth are chattering. I'd climb the curtains if there were any. I shiver from head to toe. My hair is standing straight up.

"Hey, Billy, you look like you just came out of the dryer!" Foxy cries, laughing.

I sulk. **I am offended!**

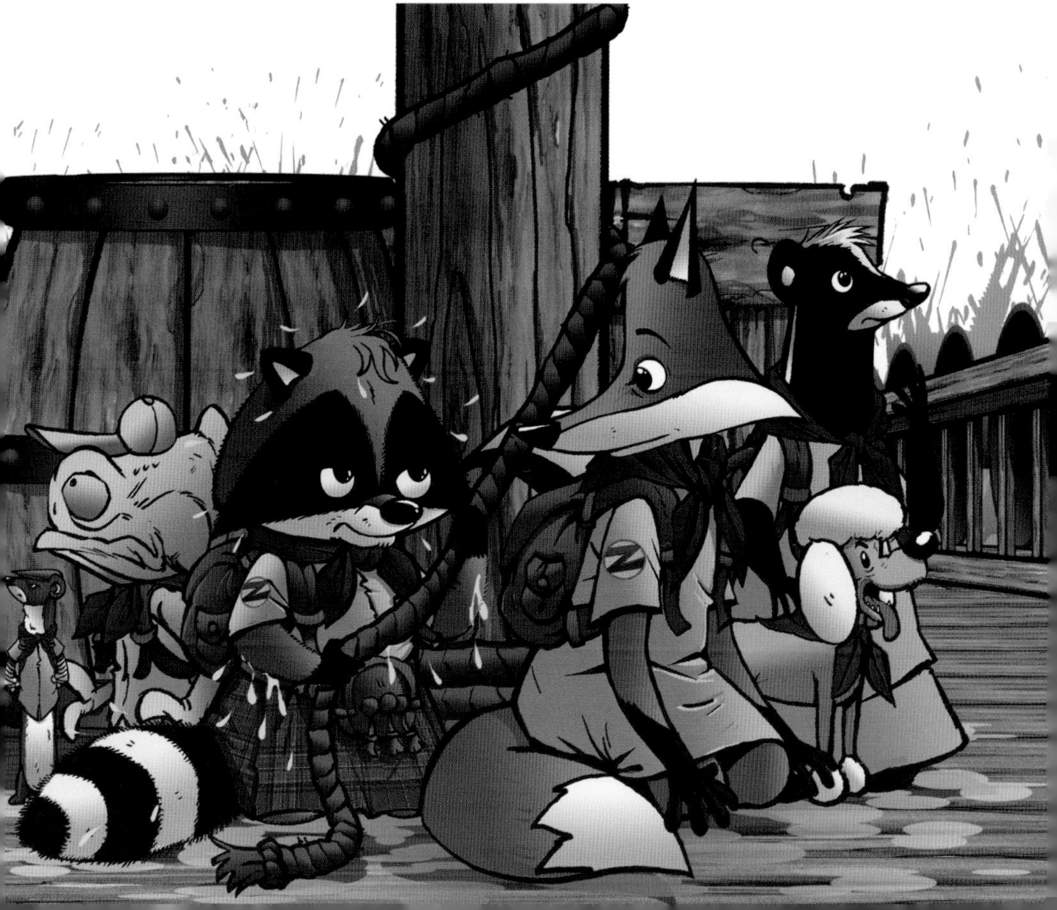

Following in my grandfather Virgil's footsteps was a BAD IDEA. But now that we're doing it, there's no time for weakness. I must set a good example for the others.

I try to reassure myself by remembering that if I see LIGHTNING FLASH and I can hear thunder, it's because I have not yet been struck by the LIGHTNING.

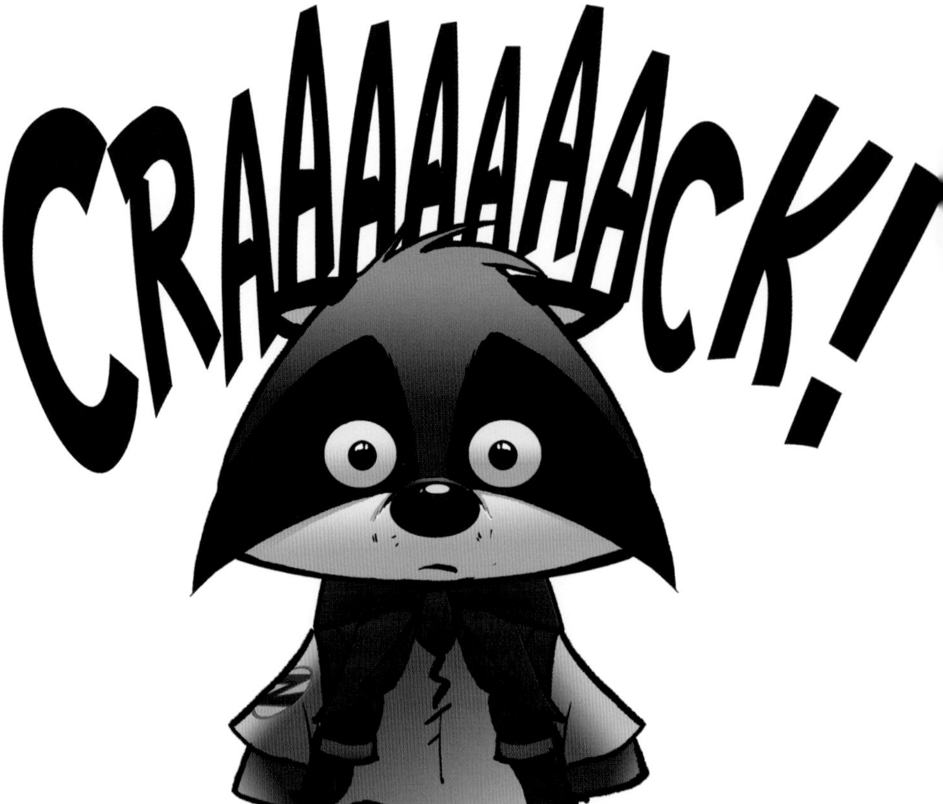
CRAAAAAAACK!

TOTAL PANIC...

I watch everyone around me. They seem more worried by the giant crashing waves, which are getting bigger and bigger, than by the increasing flashes of lightning that are striping the sky.

I clutch a mast and close my eyes. If I could, I would also close my ears to block out the racket. It's a waste of time. Even with my eyelids shut, the brilliant light from the lightning still dazzles me. I open my eyes again.

A terrible **SHAKE** rocks the boat, followed by an enormous wave that unfurls on the bridge and flips several members of the team.

"Man overboard!" cries someone.

Right away the sailor corrects himself.

"Not a man! ***Fox overboard!***"

A fox? Foxy!

She's fallen in the water!

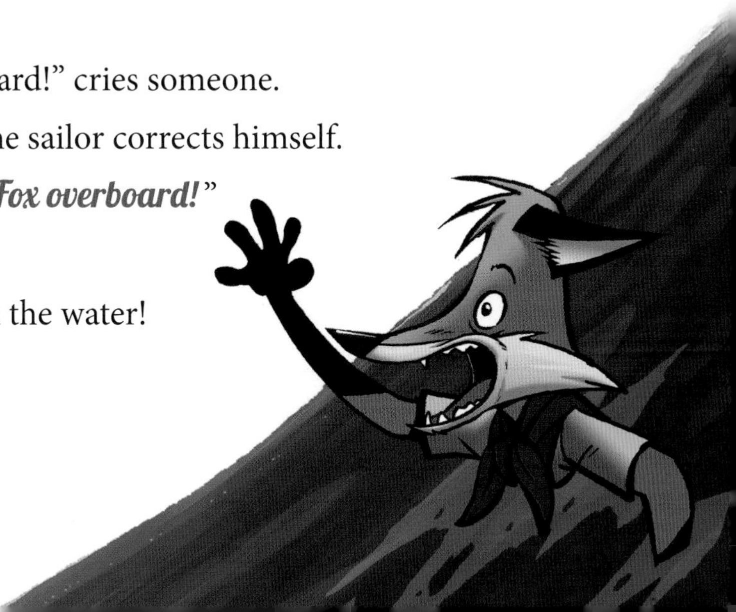

THE SHOPKEEPER'S CHALLENGE

Billy Stuart wants to buy **NINE CHOCOLATE CRAWFISH**.

The Cavendish candy-store owner gives him a challenge.

"Look closely, Billy Stuart. All the crawfish you see weigh the same except for one, which is heavier than the other eight. If you can figure out which one it is, I will give you them all. But be careful! You can only use the scale twice to succeed."

Billy licks his chops! He knows what he has to do to win the mother lode. How about you? Do you know?

Solution on page 142.

Fox Overboard!

I forget about being scared of the thunder. Foxy is out there in the sea! She is trying super hard to stay afloat. Every now and then a breaking wave swallows her up.

"Throw her a *rope!*" the captain orders.

His sister, Timoree, runs onto the bridge. She grabs a rope from the deck. At the gunwale, she throws one end of the rope overboard, aiming for Foxy. Not far enough! It's impossible for Foxy to reach it.

Quickly Timoree pulls it back in and gives it a second try. Another fail!

Unceremoniously Musky takes the rope from her and throws it in. *Touchdown!* Bravo!

"Hold on, Foxy!" cries the skunk.

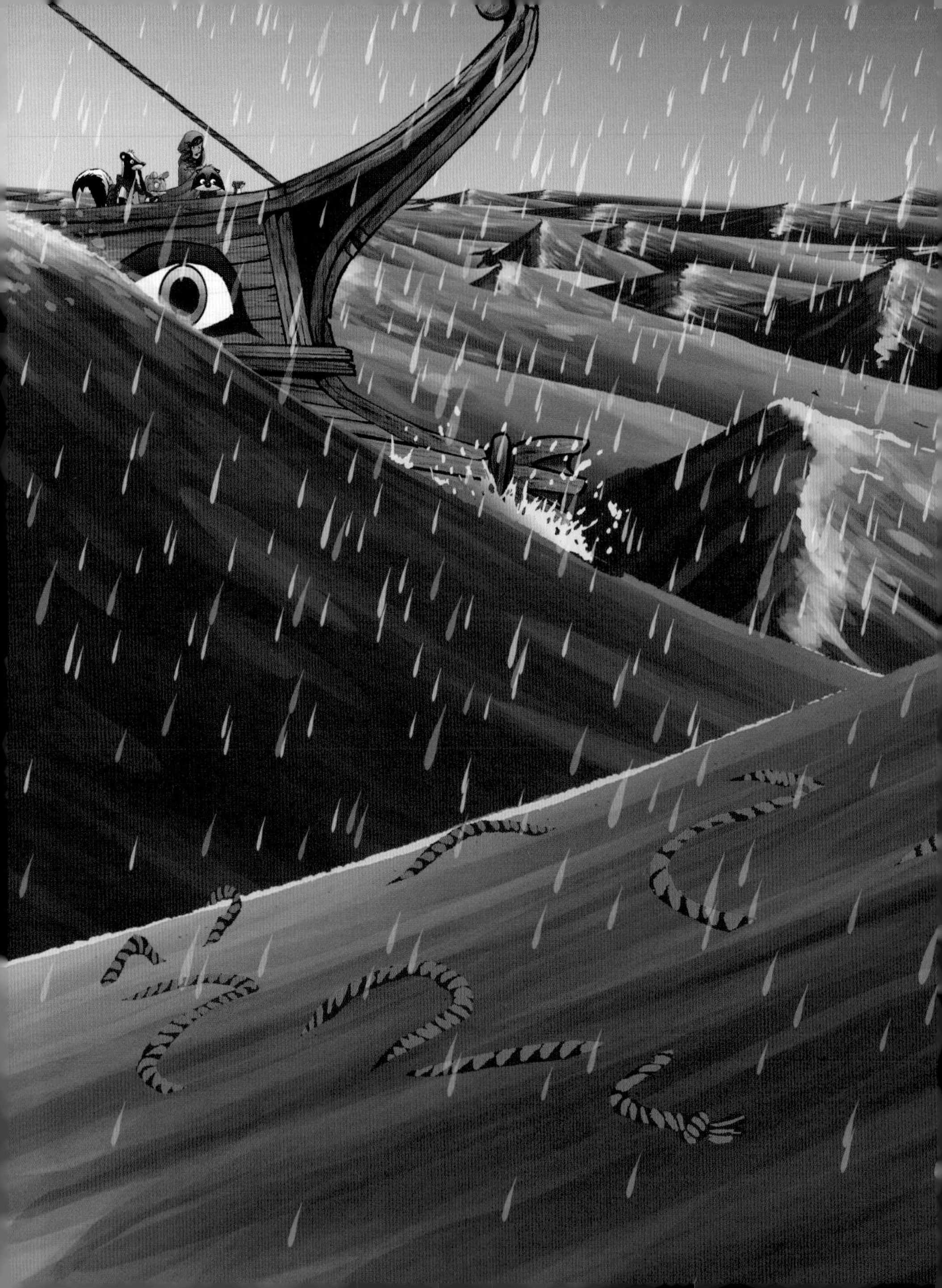

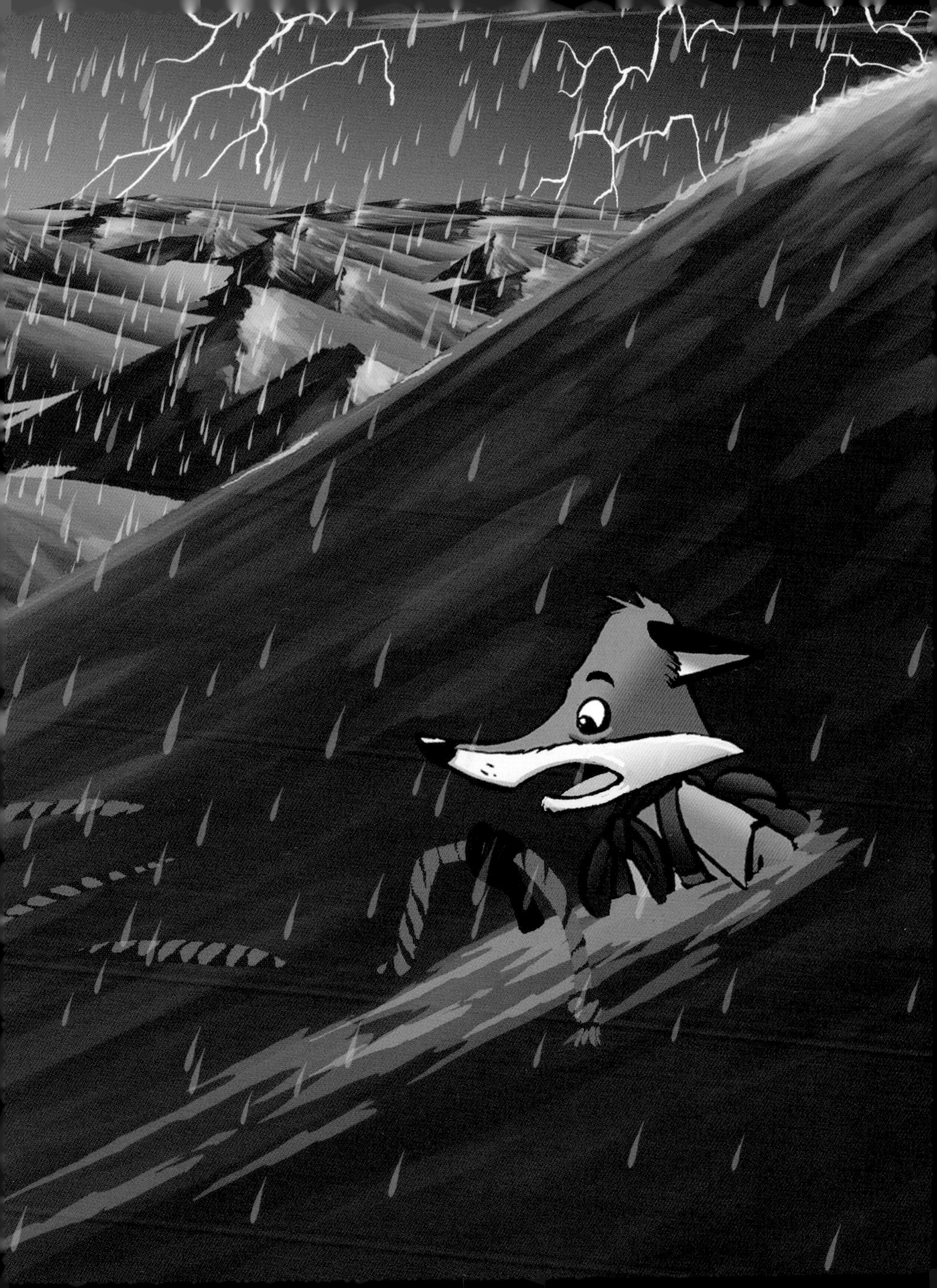

Timoree is furious. Not because Musky got it right with one throw, but because she let go of her end of the rope.

I am furious.

"Really, Musky! What were you thinking?"

"The rope slipped out of my hands, Billy Stuart," she pleads, overwhelmed and sheepish.

SPLASH!

"A little boy overboard!" yells a sailor.

And then he corrects himself.

"Not a little boy! *A weasel overboard!*"

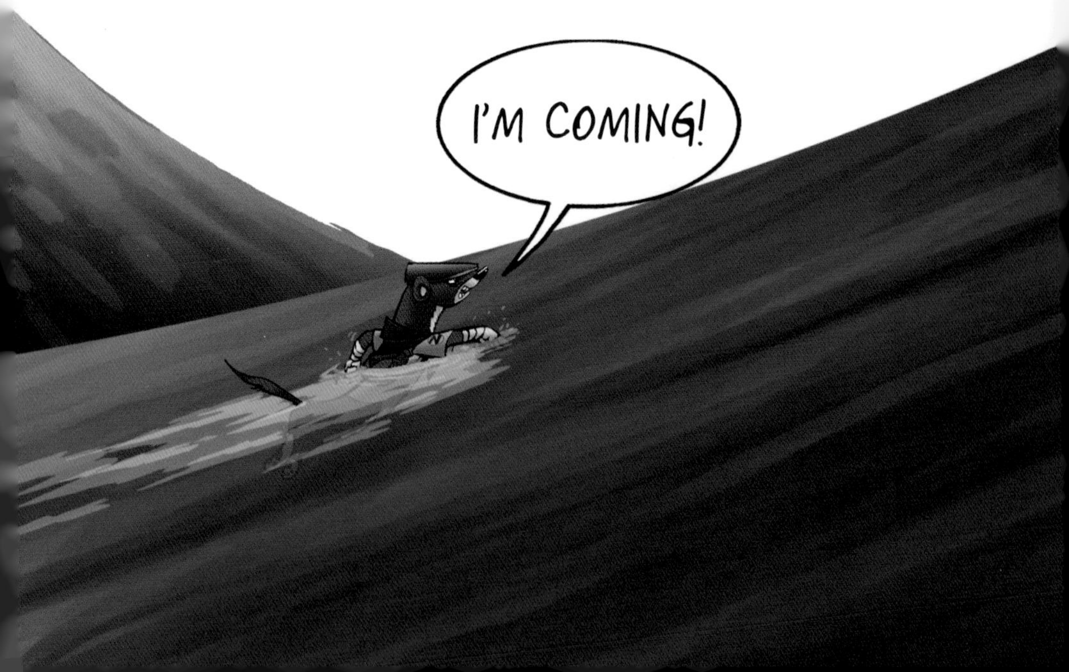
I'M COMING!

So now Yeti is also in the water. Except a wave didn't take him. He dived in to save his friend Foxy.

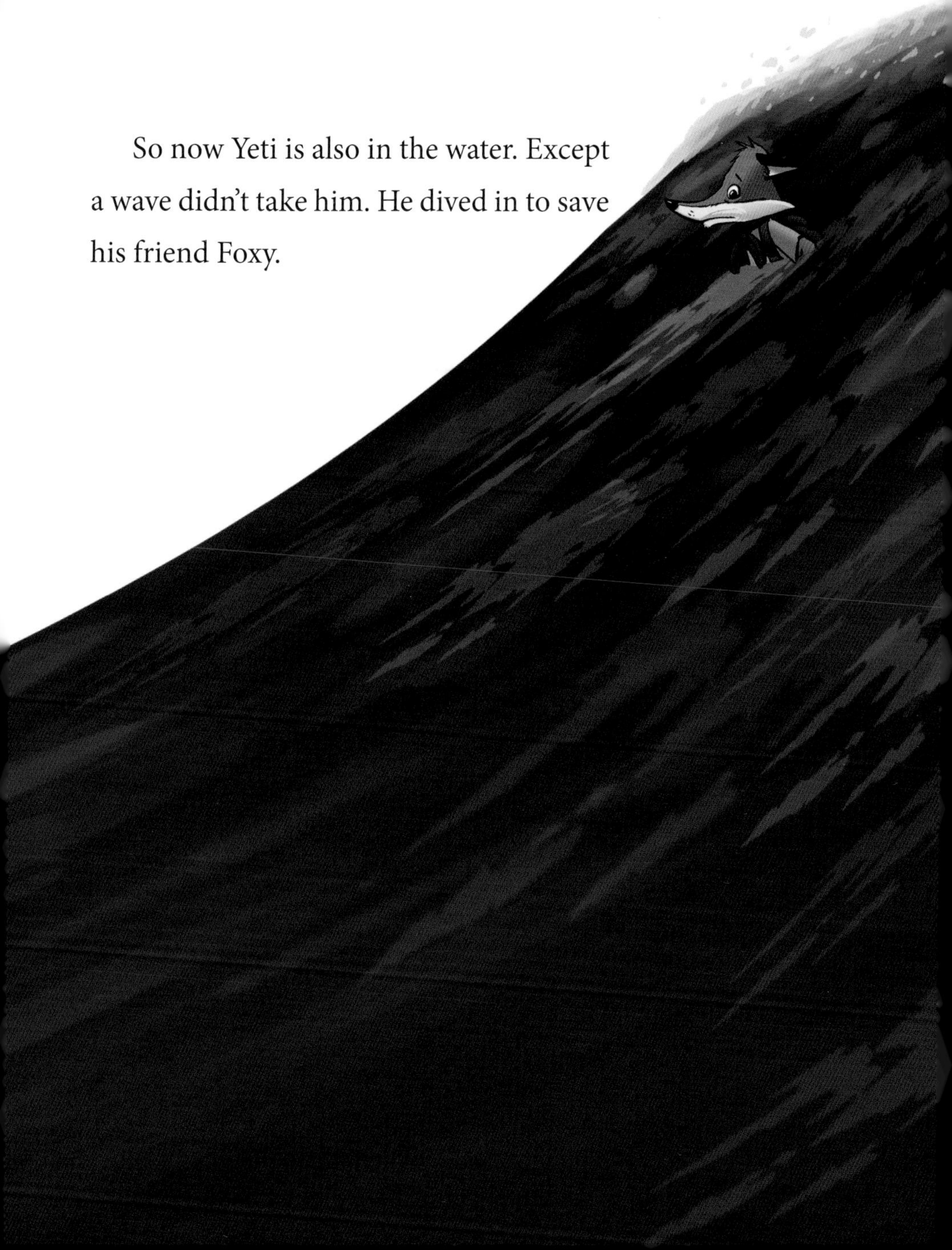

It's strange to see a weasel doing the butterfly stroke! Yeti is being tossed around like a cork out there, and he moves slowly through the waves.

I'm not worried anymore about the rolling thunder or the lightning strikes that are battering the ship. Nothing else matters except getting Foxy and Yeti to safety.

Timoree doesn't skip a beat. She runs to get another rope.

SPLASH!

"*A white rat overboard!*" cries the sailor.

And then he corrects himself.

"Not a white rat! A white dog overboard!"

That's all we need! FrouFrou has dived in to join Foxy.

I am incredulous. I stare at Shifty.

"You want to go too? Why not?"

A HUGE WAVE hits the ship, making it lean dangerously to one side. Sailors fall into the sea. Musky, Shifty and I grip the gunwale, almost plunging overboard.

Where have our friends gone?

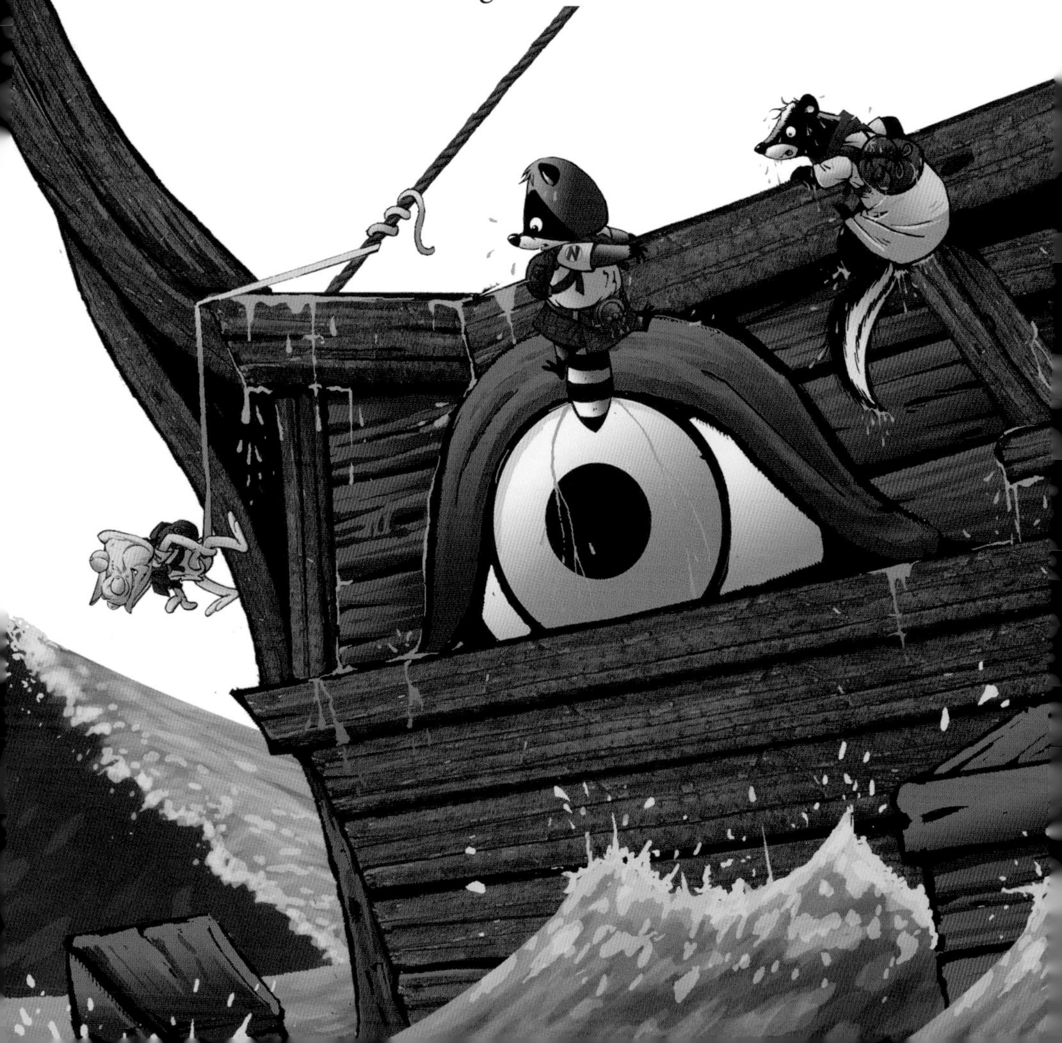

Yeti and FrouFrou make it to Foxy. I don't know how! Or maybe it's the other way around. I guess it doesn't matter. The three Zintrepids in the water swim closer to the ship. They manage to grab on to two oars and cling to them to avoid sinking.

Oars? Captain Loslobos's order earlier to bring up the oars must not have been heard. **THIS IS TERRIBLE!** Now the boat has lost all its oars!

Timoree, with impressive precision, throws the rope to the Zintrepids. Foxy seizes it while Yeti grabs the poodle's collar with one hand and the fox's arm with his other.

The captain's sister, with our help, pulls the trio toward us. The whole process is made more difficult by the ship being BATTERED on all sides by the waves. Foxy doesn't drop the rope, though, and after several long minutes the fox, the weasel and the dog are returned safe and sound to the deck of the boat.

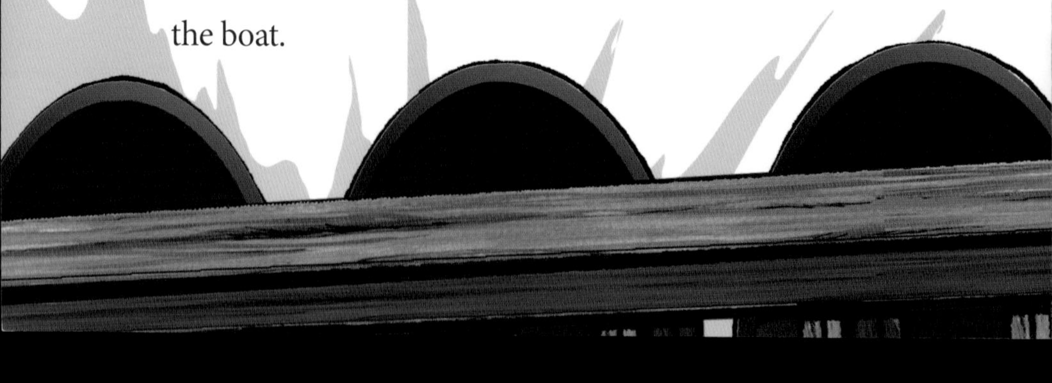

“Thanks! Phew! That was a close call!” says Foxy.

My friends vigorously shake seawater off of themselves.

“Ah!” exclaims the fox. “Feels good to be dr—”

A big wave splashes over her.

“—dry.”

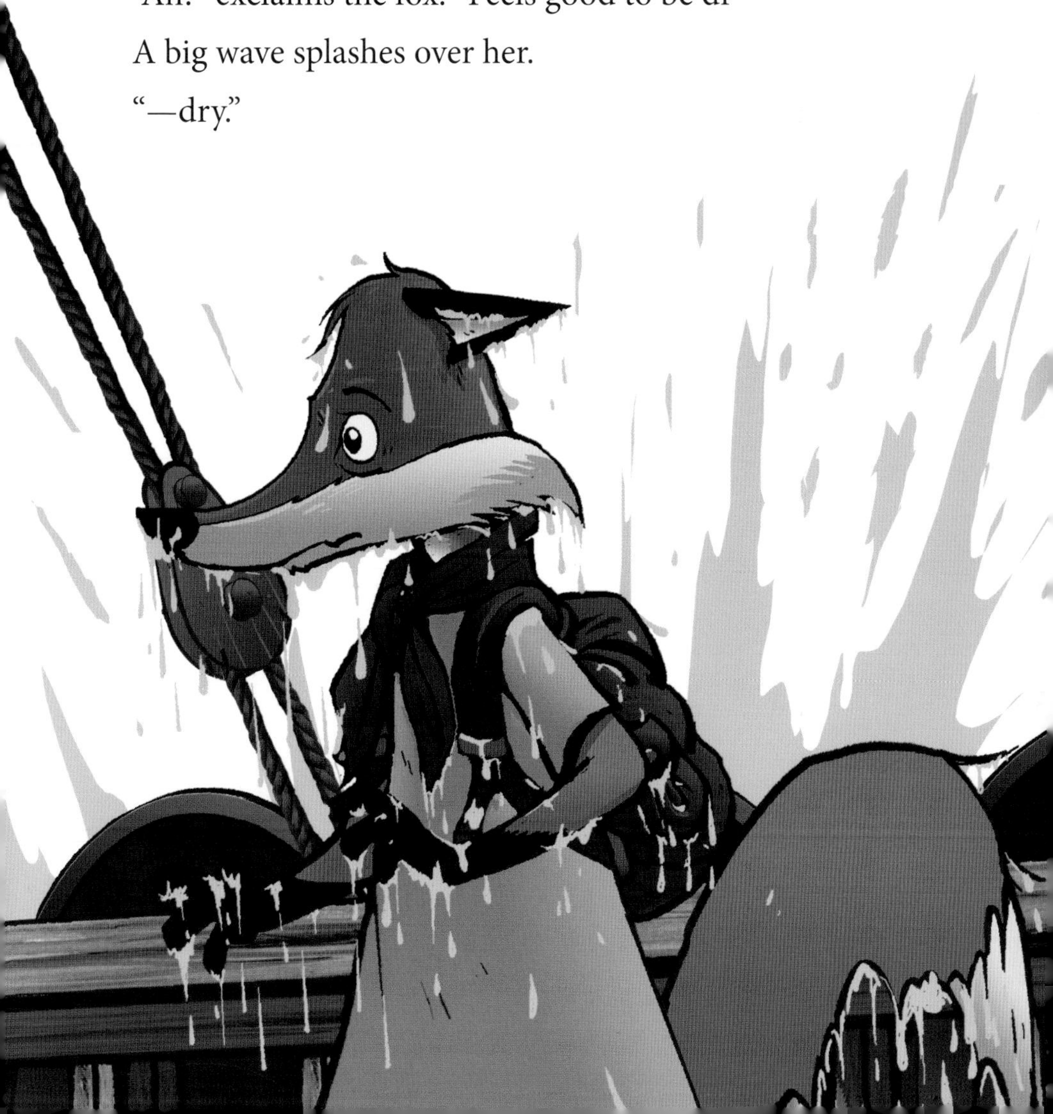

COLORS GAME

As you know, our friend Shifty, the chameleon, takes on the colors of his environment.

Here are three pots of paint.

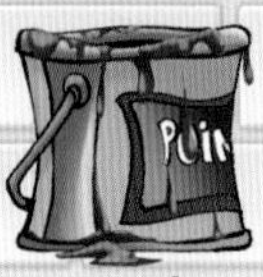

Red

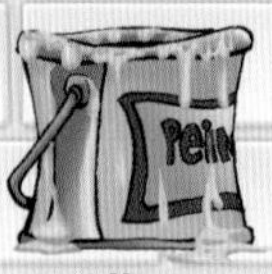

Yellow

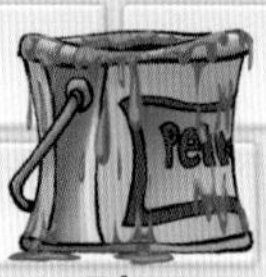

Blue

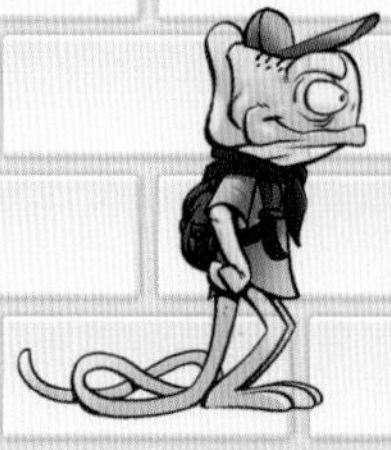

And here is our friend Shifty standing in front of a white wall.

What **colors** should I mix together to paint my wall if I want him to become **green**?

What **colors** should I use if I want Shifty to turn this pretty color of **orange**?

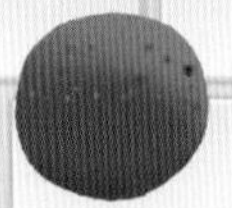

What **colors** should I use to have the wall and Shifty all **purple**?

You should mix only two colors at once.

Solution on page 143.

Chapter 4

The Calm after the Storm

Almost as quickly as it started, the storm ends. It sails past us, taking along its black **CLOUDS**, its torrents of rain, its lightning and thunder.

It is the calm after the storm.

We are now floating under a beautiful, clear blue sky.

The captain takes stock of the damage done to ship and crew. We mourn the loss of the seven sailors washed overboard. There is damage to the boat—the gunwale is in bits, and the oars are in the sea. *What will become of us now?*

We need to make the most of this calm weather to get ourselves back together and rest a bit.

Clearly, this is not the end of our troubles.

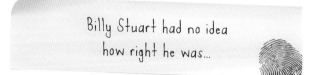

Billy Stuart had no idea
how right he was...

It really *is* the calm after the storm…

"It's flat like a board!" says Shifty, who is stretched out on the bridge.

"You're bored?" I ask, sitting beside him.

With the arrival of the LOVELY WEATHER, barely anything is happening. Our ship is practically immobile, even with the sails up.

The water is so flat it looks like **CEMENT**.

There is nothing around us—not a single spit of land where we could go ashore.

"We've been thrown considerably off course," admits Loslobos, his eyes glued to the horizon.

The slave master, Ugobos, looks grim.

"The gods are powerful, my captain. They have unleashed the elements on us. And now look at us. We are LOST in the middle of nowhere, at the mercy of the **MONSTERS** of the sea."

Loslobos flicks his hand at Ugobos.

"Nonsense! We faced a horrible storm and, despite everything, managed to stay alive. The gods weren't testing us—they were protecting us!"

Ugobos gives me **DIRTY LOOK**.

And then he speaks to the captain again:

"These strangers on the ship have attracted the wrath of heaven."

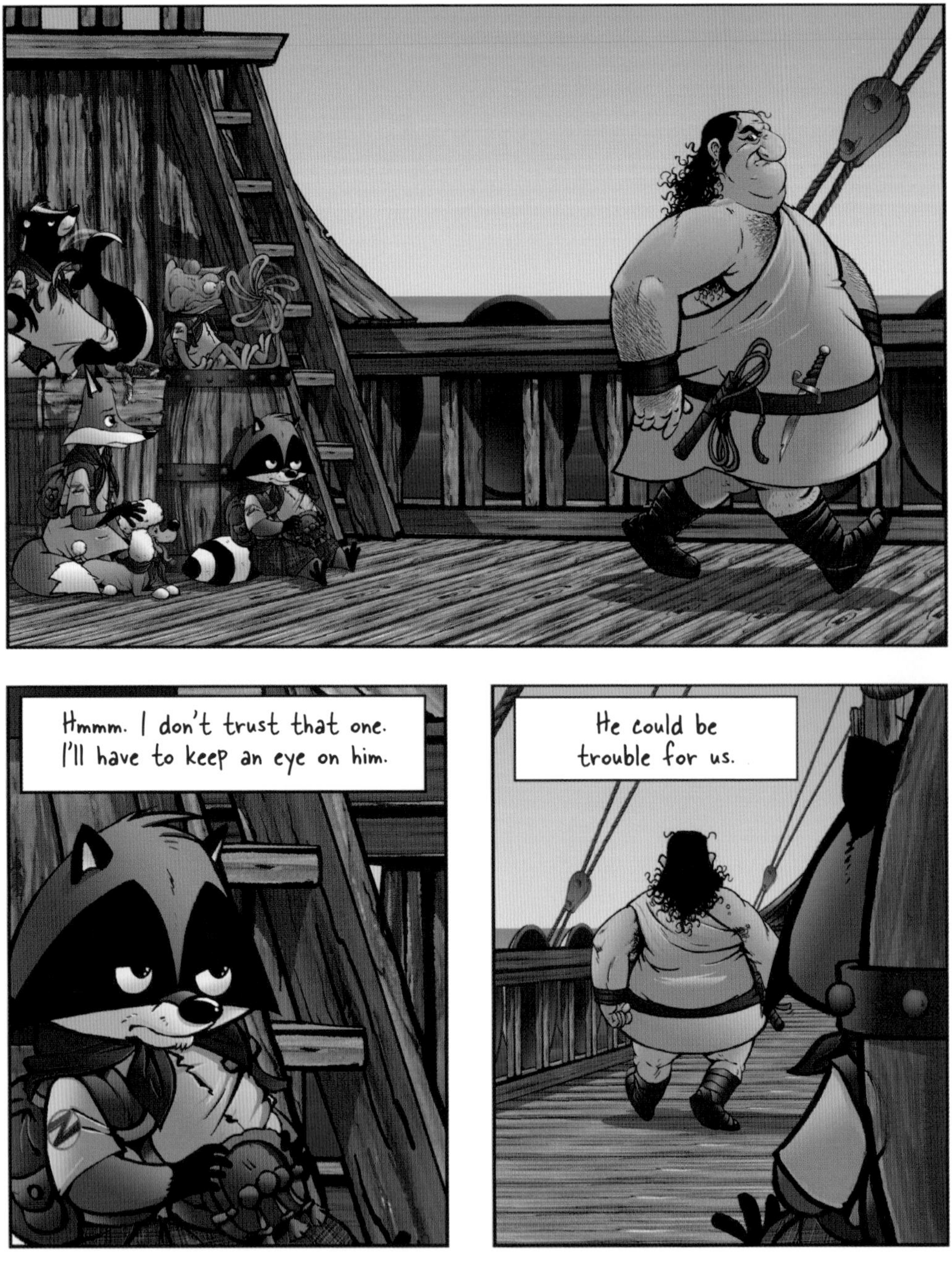
Hmmm. I don't trust that one. I'll have to keep an eye on him.
He could be trouble for us.

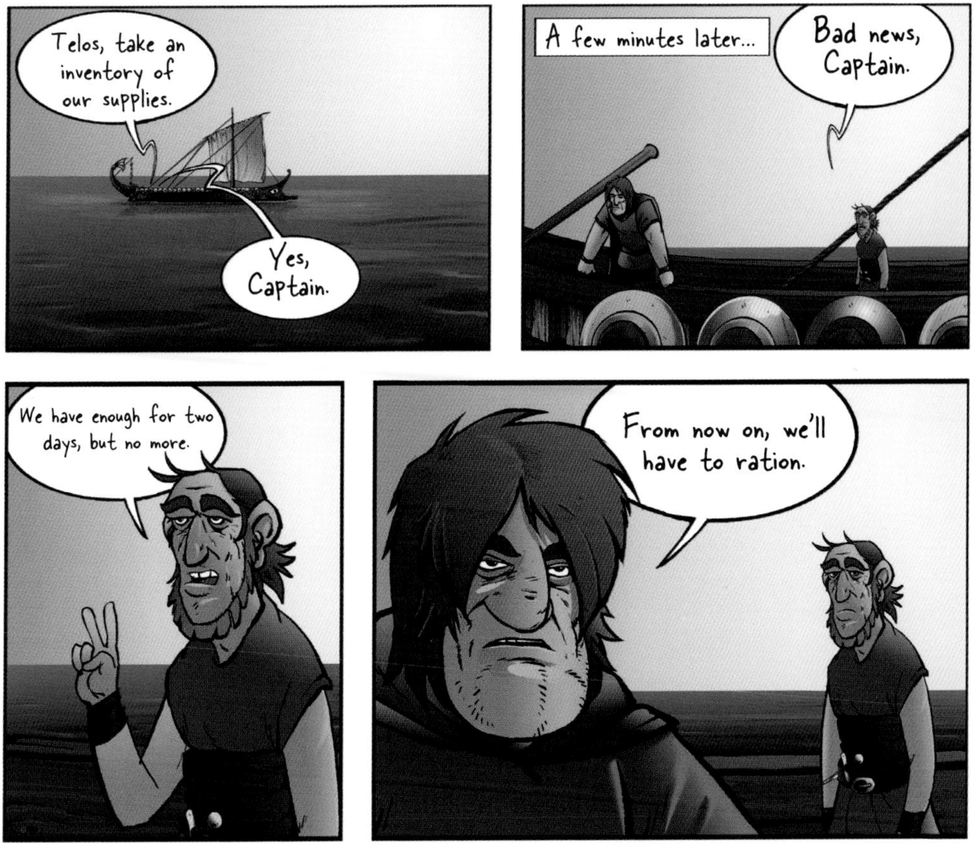
Telos, take an inventory of our supplies.
Yes, Captain.
A few minutes later...
Bad news, Captain.
We have enough for two days, but no more.
From now on, we'll have to ration.

Yet again, Billy Stuart is a prophet. He saw this coming.

As if he's talking to himself, he says, "And we don't know when the wind will come back."

At my feet, FrouFrou barks to get my attention. He's hungry. Foxy takes care of it. She rummages in her bag and finds him a few TREATS.

I remind her to manage her provisions carefully.

"You never know…"

In the sky, the SUN shines like a thousand fires. If feels like a menacing force above our heads, planning our demise. Poker-face Ugobos, the slave master, is talking quietly with the crew nearby. This doesn't bode well.

Growing Discontent

We don't know exactly why, but the crew's mood has turned sour, and several sailors are eyeing us in a **SUSPICIOUS** manner. Us! The Zintrepids!

They are blaming us for their MISFORTUNE.

I have no proof, but I think Ugobos is telling them this is all our fault.

Suddenly this boat feels super cramped.

Days and days go by, and the ship doesn't seem to move an inch. After screaming at us for hours, the wind just left to **BLOW** elsewhere.

The provisions are almost all gone, fishing has been unsuccessful, and fresh water is scarce. A nice shower would be welcome!

Timoree comes over to say hi. She pats FrouFrou's head, and he gets excited. And then PEES everywhere!

I tell Timoree my worries about the crew.

She tries to reassure me.

"As long as my brother is captain, there's nothing to worry about. The men highly respect him."

At that moment, a **HEATED DISCUSSION** breaks out at the front of the boat. Loslobos stands facing a group of sailors led by Ugobos. We go up to see what's going on. Ugobos is speaking the loudest and leading the charge.

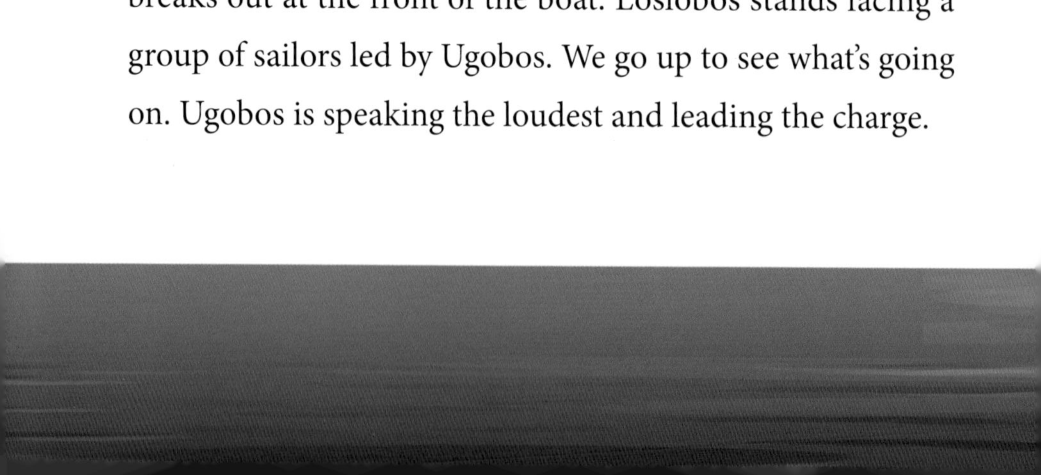

"The gods of the wind and the sea are demanding sacrifices. We must satisfy their DESIRES. If we don't, we risk provoking their fury and dying here, far from our families."

Aeolus is the god of the winds. Poseidon is the god of the sea. Poseidon is also the name of a ship that was toppled over by a giant wave in a disaster movie called *The Poseidon Adventure*. When I saw that movie, it blew me away.

As soon as he's raised the idea of SACRIFICES, Ugobos designates us, and since he's gotten us in the bad books of the others, they approve. The captain holds steady.

"*ENOUGH!* Sacrifices won't change one bit of our situation."

"I say they will!" replies Ugobos.

With one quick move, he gets behind Loslobos and puts a knife to his throat.

Mutiny in the Morning

This morning's mutiny must have been planned. As soon as Ugobos puts a knife to the captain's throat, his men seize Timoree and us. We have nothing to defend ourselves with.

"Bring it on! No, really, bring *it* on!" Yeti challenges, punching his **LITTLE FISTS** into empty air.

A sailor lifts him up by his collar, holding him at bay.

"Sorry, Captain, but you leave us with no choice," says Ugobos with a **NASTY SMILE**.

Excited by all this action, the poodle dances on his hind legs and barks.

"Stupid dog," I mutter in frustration. "CLEAR OFF! Go jump in the sea!"

 43

FrouFrou responds by sitting down with his mouth hanging open, tongue swinging, waiting to see what will happen next.

"What will you do with us?" Foxy demands anxiously.

"You are the source of all our PROBLEMS," Ugobos says. "We will sacrifice you to appease Aeolus's fury and save ourselves from any more trouble. Thank you!"

"The pleasure is all ours," Foxy replies sarcastically.

We are taken to the back of the SHIP, where a floorboard has been pulled up and is now perched on the gunwale, one end suspended out over the sea.

WALK THE PLANK!

There is no way out. The sailors outnumber us. The captain and Timoree are being held prisoner. Running away? To where? The sea? Ah! The scoundrels have planned this well.

I don't think my grandfather Virgil expected such an outcome for our adventure.

The sailor ties our hands behind our backs. The rope is so tight that it's cutting off my circulation.

Ugobos is chomping at the bit.

"Who should we start with?"

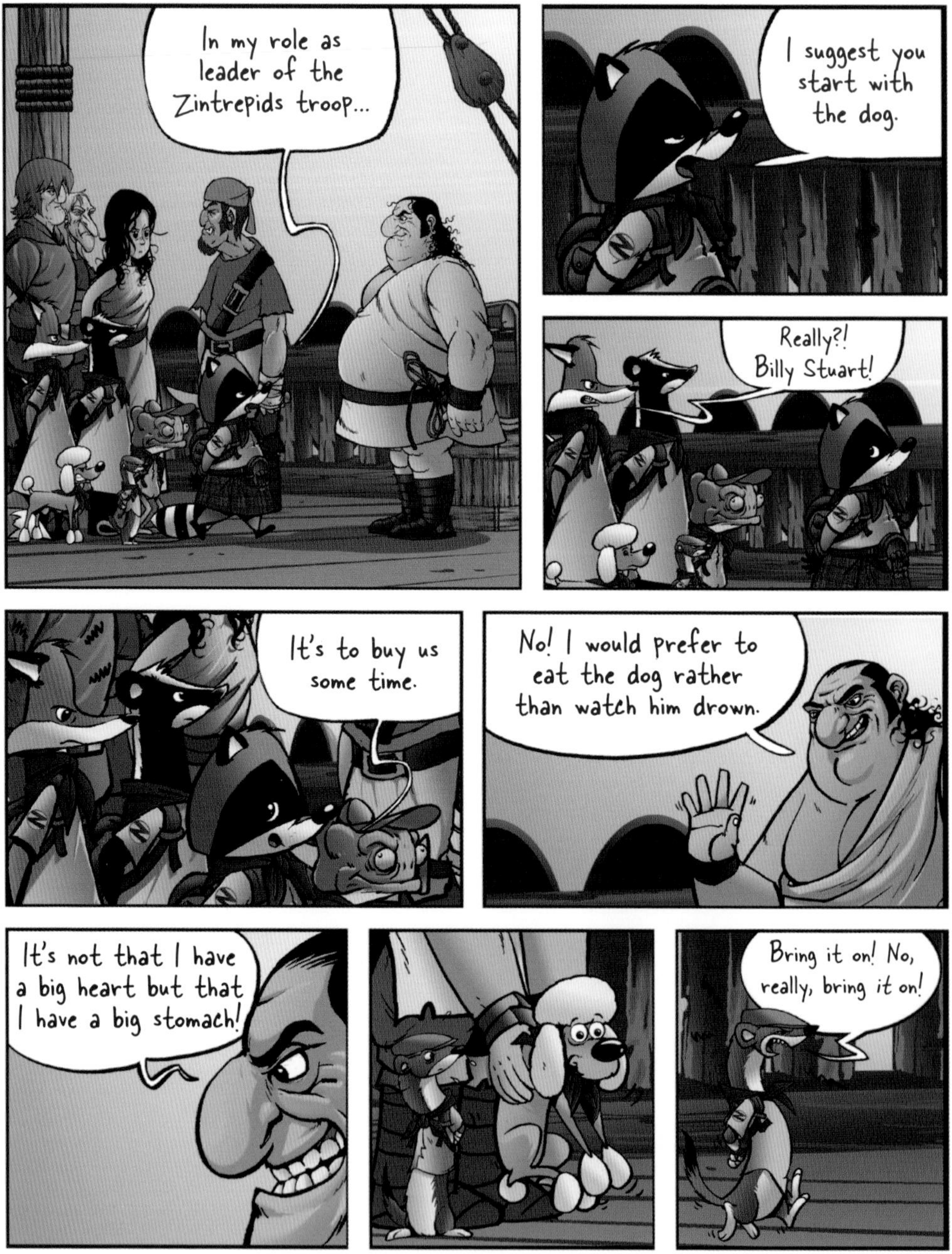
In my role as leader of the Zintrepids troop...
I suggest you start with the dog.
Really?! Billy Stuart!
It's to buy us some time.
No! I would prefer to eat the dog rather than watch him drown.
It's not that I have a big heart but that I have a big stomach!
Bring it on! No, really, bring it on!

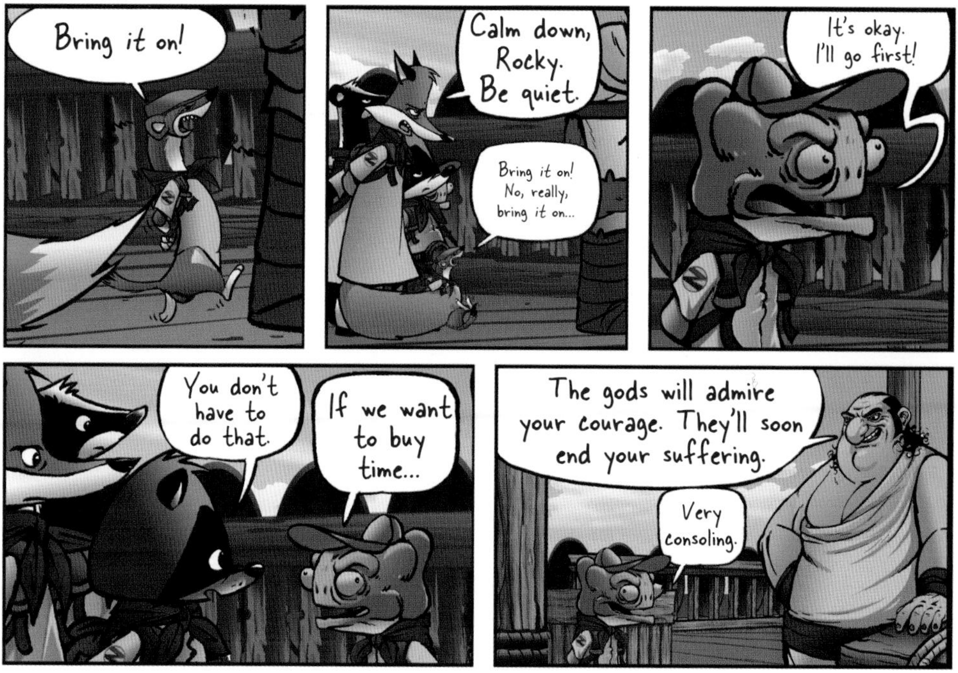
Bring it on!
Calm down, Rocky. Be quiet.
Bring it on! No, really, bring it on...
It's okay. I'll go first!
You don't have to do that.
If we want to buy time...
The gods will admire your courage. They'll soon end your suffering.
Very consoling.

Slowly the chameleon climbs onto the plank. He takes two steps forward, one step back, two steps forward, one step back, until he reaches the end.

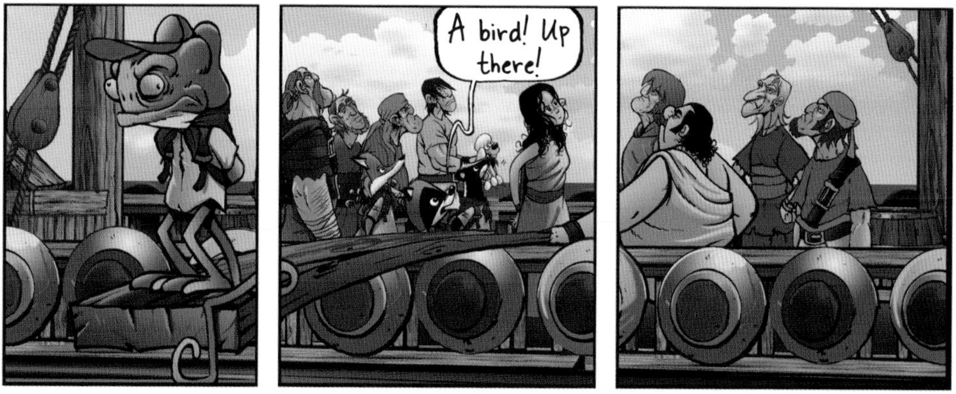
A bird! Up there!

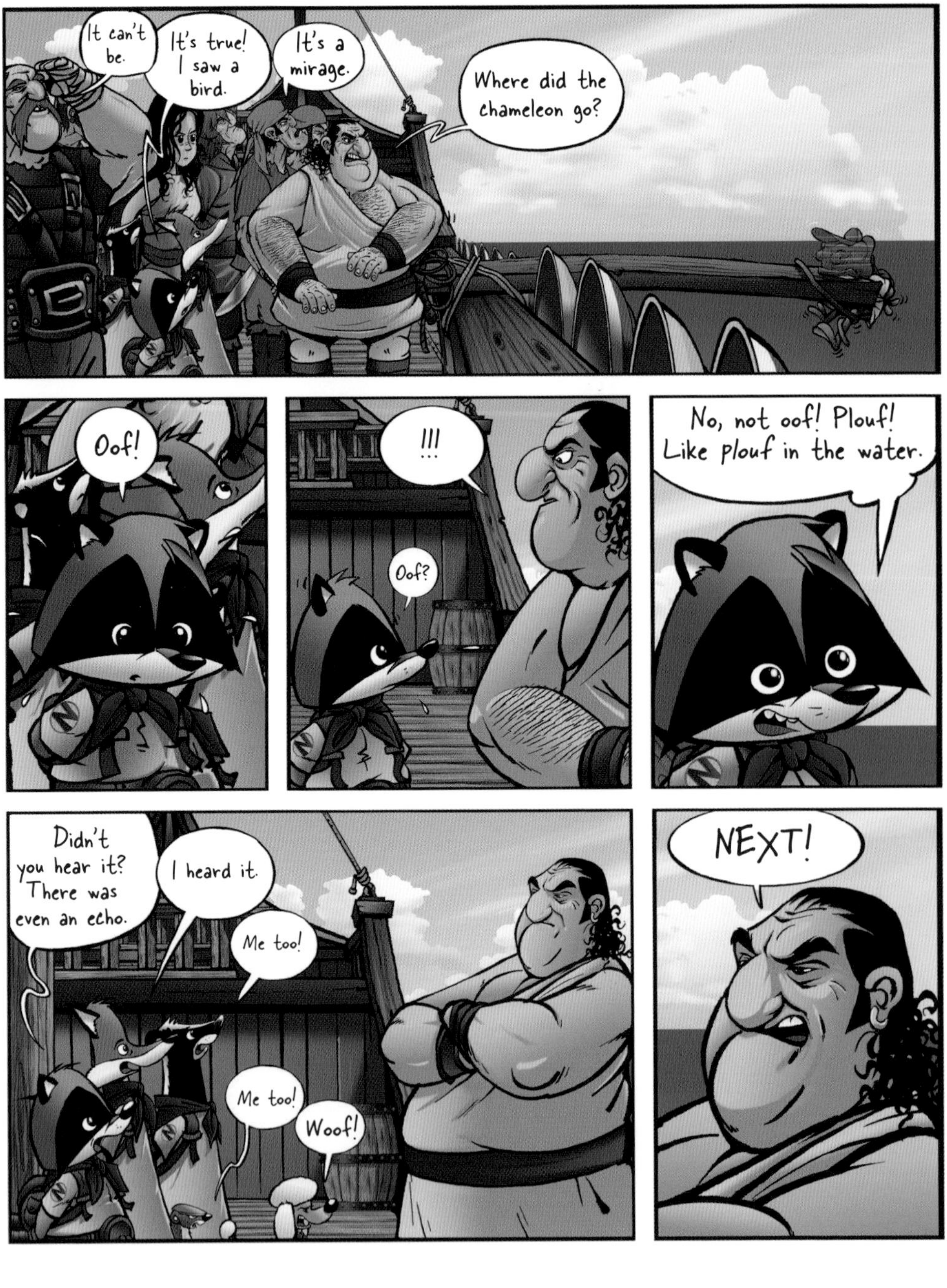
It can't be.
It's true! I saw a bird.
It's a mirage.
Where did the chameleon go?
Oof!
!!!
Oof?
No, not oof! Plouf! Like plouf in the water.
Didn't you hear it? There was even an echo.
I heard it.
Me too!
Me too!
Woof!
NEXT!

Chapter 7

My Turn

I didn't mean to create a diversion. I really had seen a bird. At the very least, the animal had feathers and was an unusual size. Maybe it was a **UFO**.

Unidentified birds often get confused with Unidentified Flying Objects (UFOS).

I'm not an ornithologist—a bird specialist. What I appreciate about birds is their eggs! YUM! YUM!

"You with the skirt! You're next," Ugobos yells at me.

"It's not a skirt, mister. It's a kilt."

What a buffoon!

I throw my companions a last glance. As I walk to my fate, my legs **TREMBLE**.

As I walk, I am careful not to step on Shifty, who is still in the same spot. I get to the end of the PLANK.

A gentle wind caresses my face as I cry:

"I am the king of the Woooooorrrrrllllld!"

This is a famous line from the movie *Titanic*, directed by James Cameron and starring Leonardo DiCaprio as Jack, and Kate Winslet as Rose. Ask your parents.

I lift a leg and start to jump.

Wait! The wind on my face?

The wind! Am I feeling things?

No! It's true! The wind is blowing!

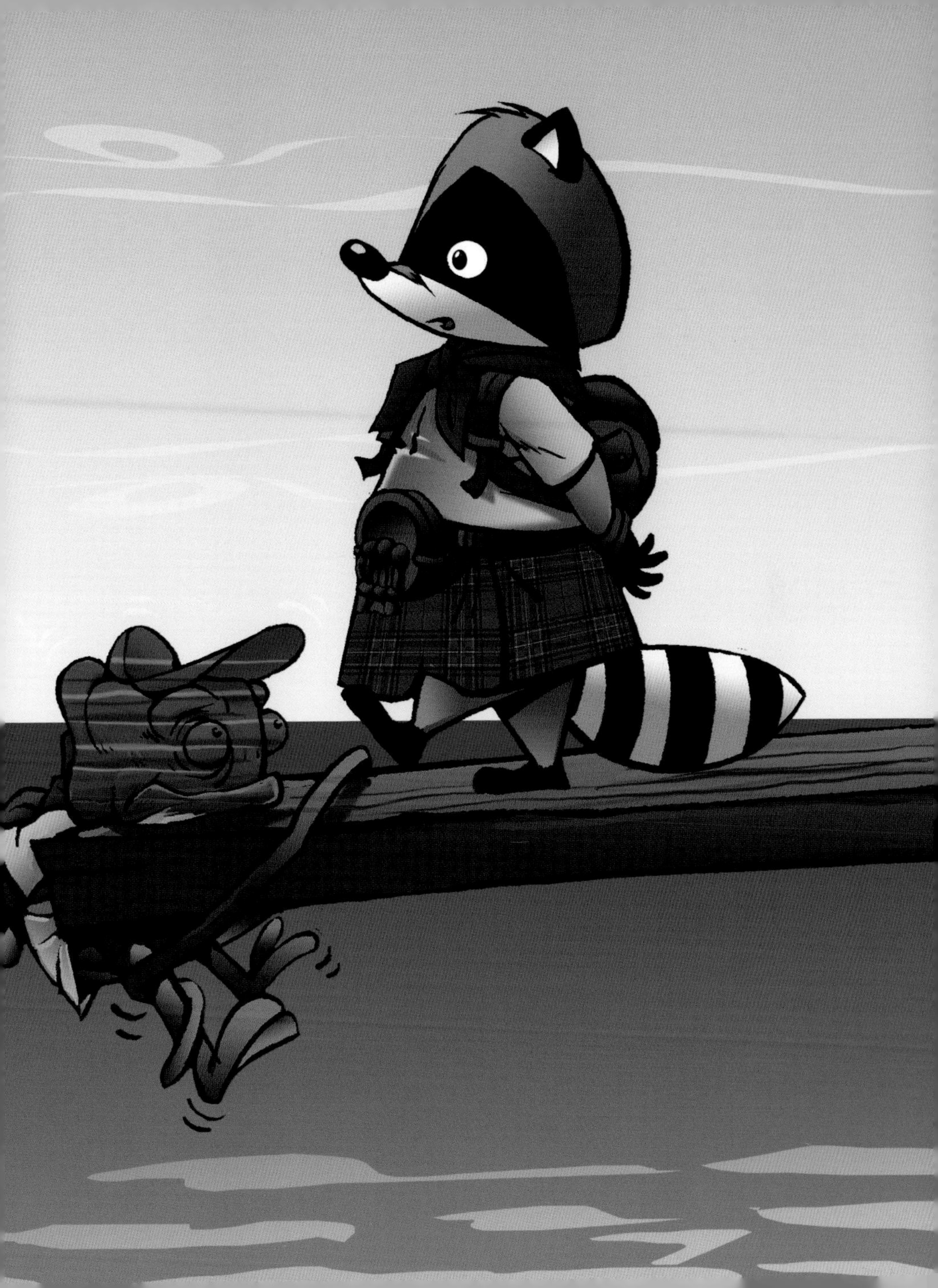

I turn to face Ugobos with a small smile on my face.

"Your god Aeolus is appeased. Look! There is WIND in the sail."

Suspicious at first, Ugobos's men eventually realize I'm right.

"YES! The wind has returned!" they shout. "We are saved!"

Ugobos splits off from the crowd and storms over to us. It's clear he'll spare me no mercy, Aeolus or no Aeolus.

I am indignant. "Don't do this! Aeolus isn't demanding more!"

Teeth CLENCHED, Ugobos comes closer.

"I'd prefer not to take any chances."

Hands extended, he prepares to throw me overboard— but trips. Shifty has stuck his foot out. The chief of the mutiny loses his balance and falls.

SPLASH!

"Hey, watch where you're going!" grumbles the chameleon, who is back to his natural **COLORS**.

Not only is the wind filling the sail, it's also turned in our favor. Captain Loslobos seizes this opportunity to take back control of the ship. He grabs a sword, points it at the crew and gives them a **STERN LOOK**.

"Sailors, either you are with me and you stay onboard, or you are against me and you can go…elsewhere."

"**HELP!!!**" yells Ugobos, who is having a hard time keeping his head above water.

"Float on your back!" Shifty yells down to him.

The men put away their weapons. They don't need to consult with one another.

"We are with you, Captain!"

A Bomb!

If misery loves company, why can't happiness have a few buddies too?

After regaining control of the crew, Loslobos orders them to *FISH* that **POISONOUS** ☠ villain Ugobos out of the water.

The slave master is made a prisoner and confined to the hold.

The rudder is fixed, and with the wind blowing generously in the sails, we steer a course toward the east.

It only takes a few hours for a drizzle to replenish our supply of fresh water.

And—the icing on the cake—the ship then comes upon a school of fish, and the fishing is incredible. The sailors get some catches as *BIIIIIIIIIIIIIG* as this!

All is going well…

All is going really well…

All is going too well…

It's not that Billy Stuart is a pessimist. Far from it. You have to remember the name of this book: *The Sea of a Thousand Dangers*. At this stage of the story, when we haven't even made it halfway through, we can count on one hand the dangers they've seen so far.

Daily routines on the ship resume. Tensions ease now that we have more food and water.

I walk FrouFrou. Foxy keeps me company.

"You seem worried, Billy Stuart," she remarks.

I hunch my shoulders.

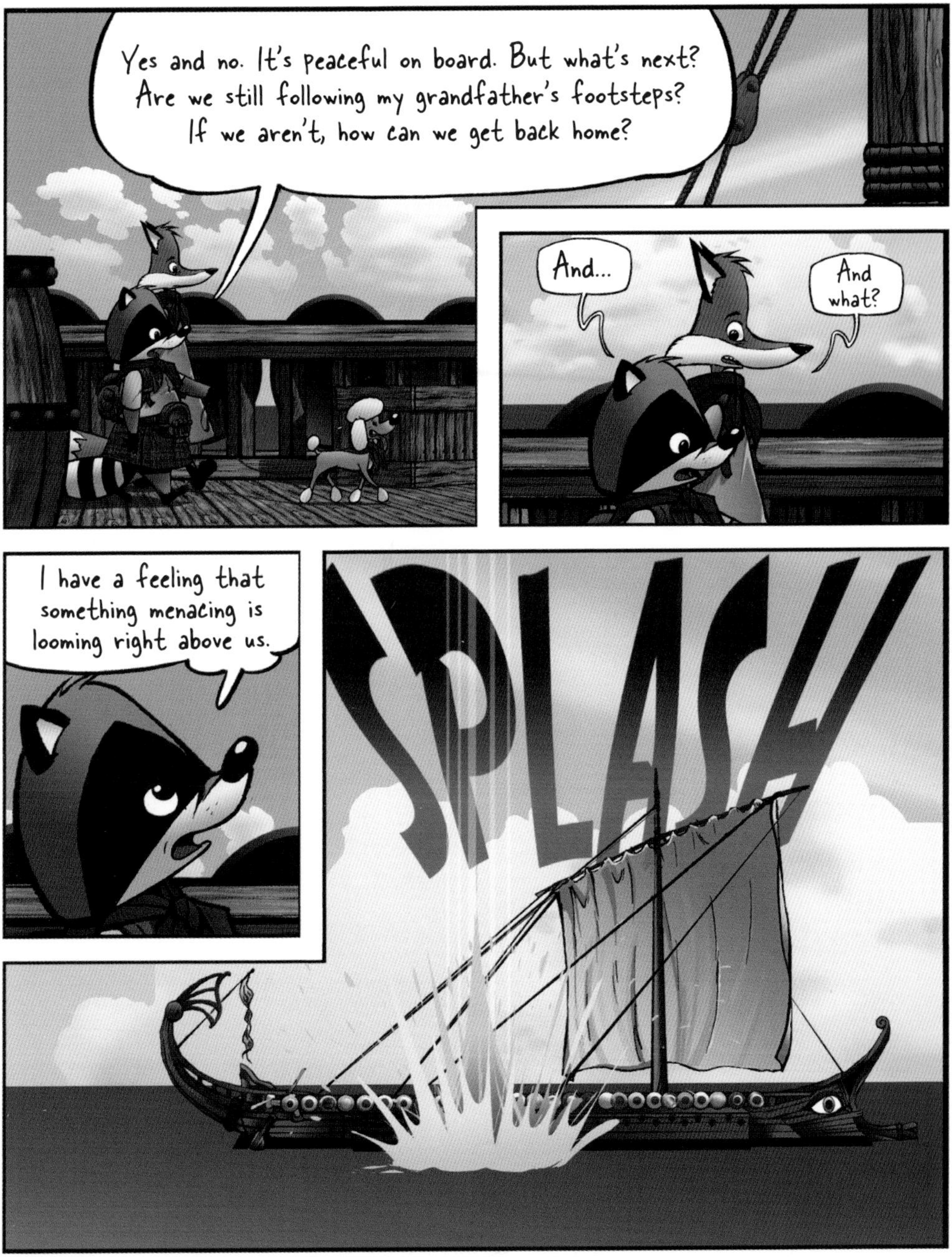
Yes and no. It's peaceful on board. But what's next? Are we still following my grandfather's footsteps? If we aren't, how can we get back home?
And...
And what?
I have a feeling that something menacing is looming right above us.
SPLASH

Something enormous has just hit the surface of the water near the boat and completely soaked us. UGH! Salty water!

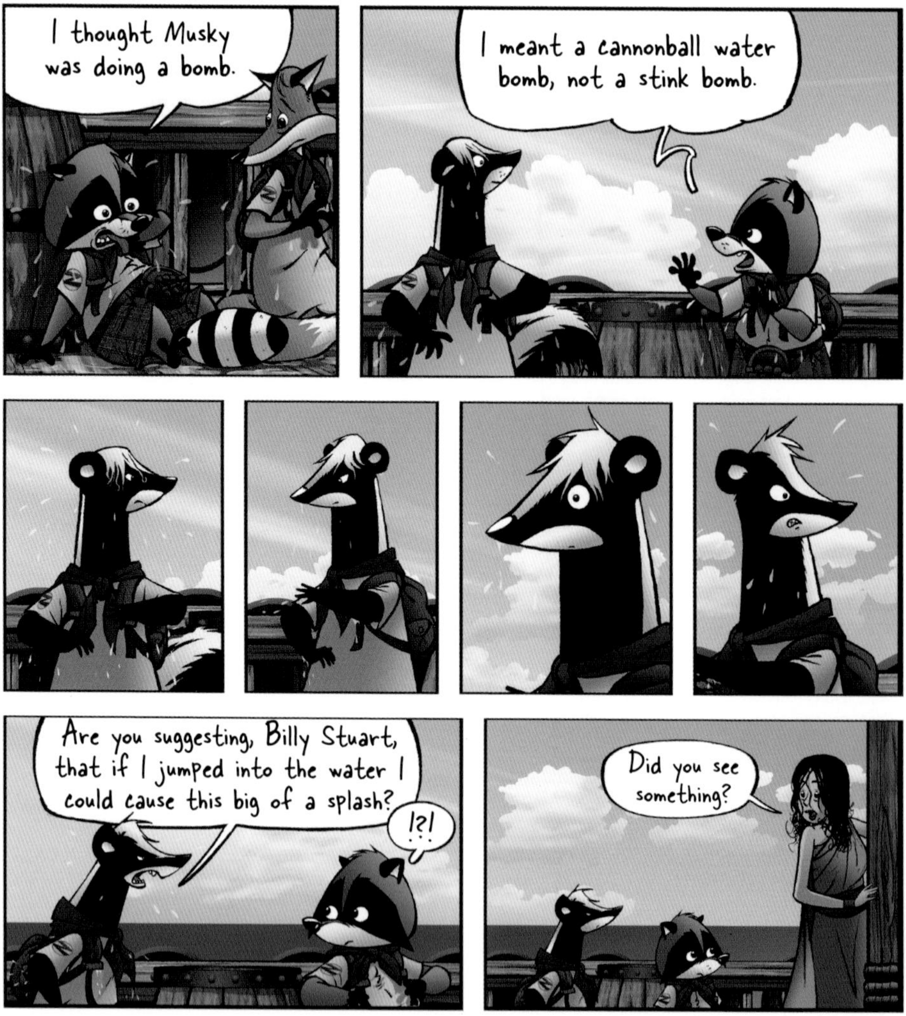

I thought Musky was doing a bomb.
I meant a cannonball water bomb, not a stink bomb.
Are you suggesting, Billy Stuart, that if I jumped into the water I could cause this big of a splash?
!?!
Did you see something?

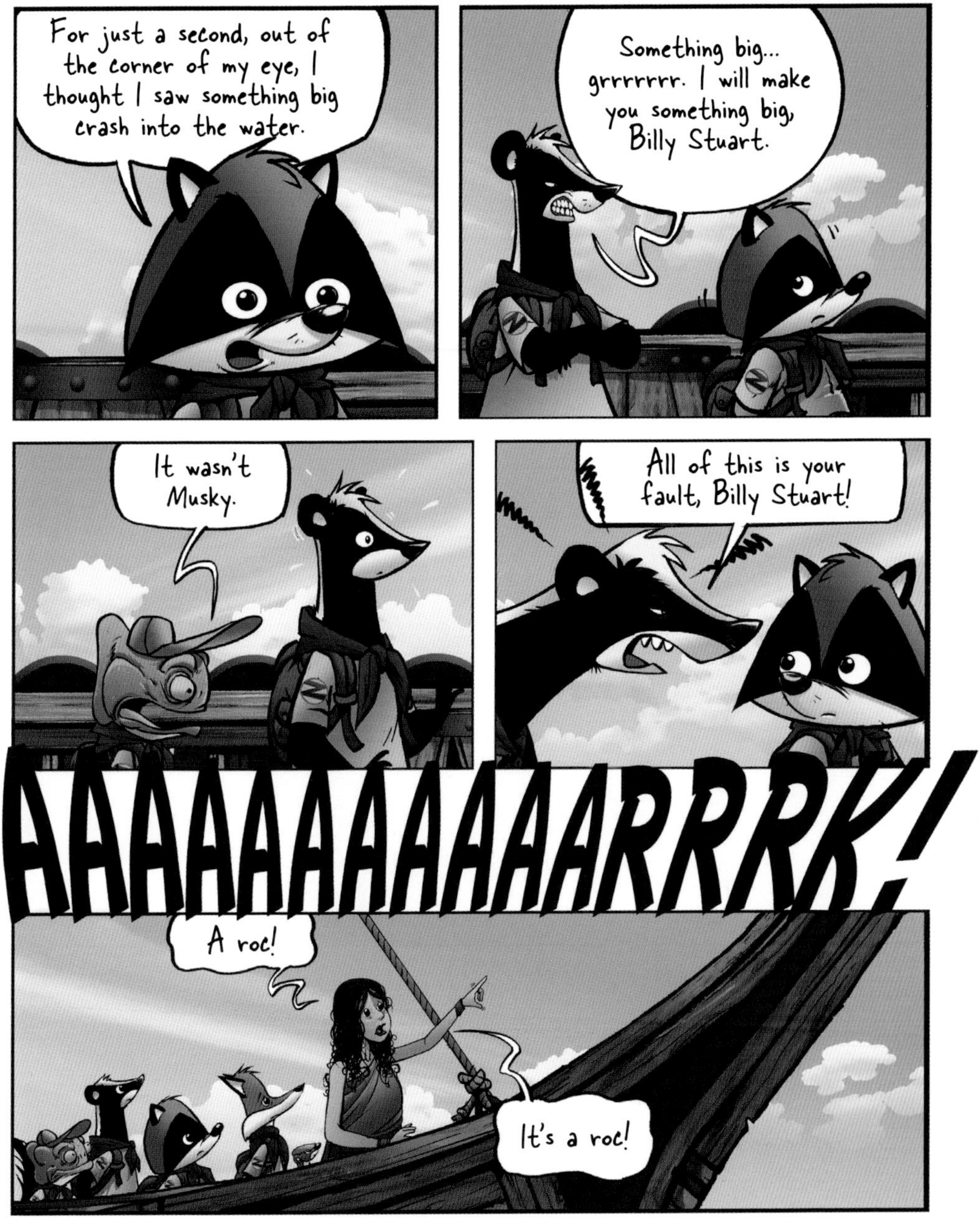
For just a second, out of the corner of my eye, I thought I saw something big crash into the water.
Something big... grrrrrrr. I will make you something big, Billy Stuart.
It wasn't Musky.
All of this is your fault, Billy Stuart!
AAAAAAAAAAARRRK!
A roc!
It's a roc!

A monstrous bird is flying toward the ship. There is a big stone, practically a boulder, in one of his claws. **OH NO!** He's throwing it in our direction!

The roc is bombing us!

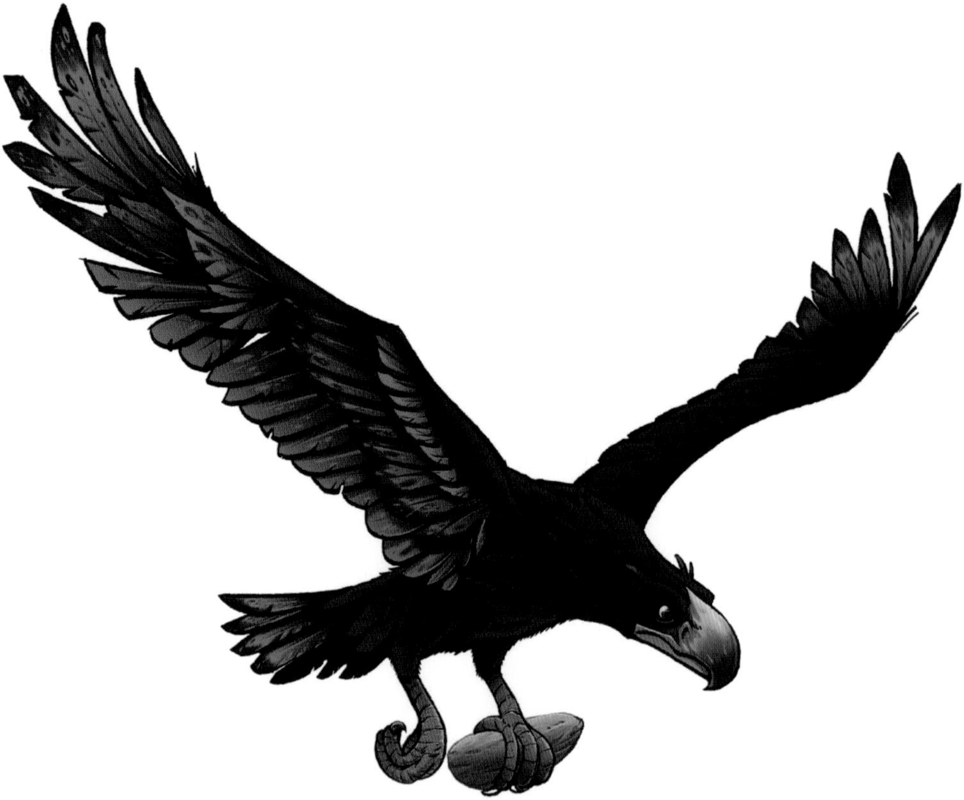

Chapter 9

Take Cover!

Let's briefly recap. While Shifty was walking the plank, I cried out, "A bird! Up there!"

Given that memory can be short, see chapter 6.

I hadn't done it just to create a diversion while Shifty blended into his surroundings. It was also because I really had seen a bird. It had seemed enormous to me and had flown in front of the SUN and suddenly disappeared. It wasn't an illusion, or a mirage, or a hallucination, or a figment of my imagination…

AAAAAAAAAAAAAAAARK!

This cry seems to be the bird equivalent of our "Here it comes!" The monster is aiming straight for our boat. If the boulder hits the ship, it will shatter the deck, and we'll all be doomed.

At the helm, Loslobos executes an emergency maneuver. Our vessel veers slowly to the .

I'm convinced it's too late. That this is it for Billy Stuart's adventures.

I wait for the shock.

SPLASH!

Splash? When a big stone hits a wooden structure, it goes CRACCCCK! Not SPLASH!

Loslobos's move has worked! The bird has failed. The whole crew breathes a sigh of relief.

That was close…

With no more ammunition, the roc, which looks like a colossal eagle and is black as a crow, cries in frustration.

AAAAAAAAAARRRK!

He flies away, beating his wings vigorously.

Is he going to find new rocks to sink us with?

"We should go in the opposite direction and try to put some distance between us," someone yells.

Loslobos, an experienced navigator, doesn't agree.

"**FOLLOW HIM!**" he cries from the helm.

Seeing the incredulous looks of his men, he explains that the bird must have a nest on an island—somewhere we could go ashore.

"Birds take the shortest possible way to the nearest landmass—they move in a straight line. That's where we must head."

The elements work in our favor. Aeolus is good to us, and the sail is STRETCHED TO ITS MAX. I would be curious to know our speed in knots.

Knots are a measure of nautical speed. One knot is equivalent to one nautical mile, which is 1.85 kilometers per hour.

Suddenly our ship collides with a SANDBAR, which stops it in its tracks. The impact throws some sailors onto land, and some fall into the sea.

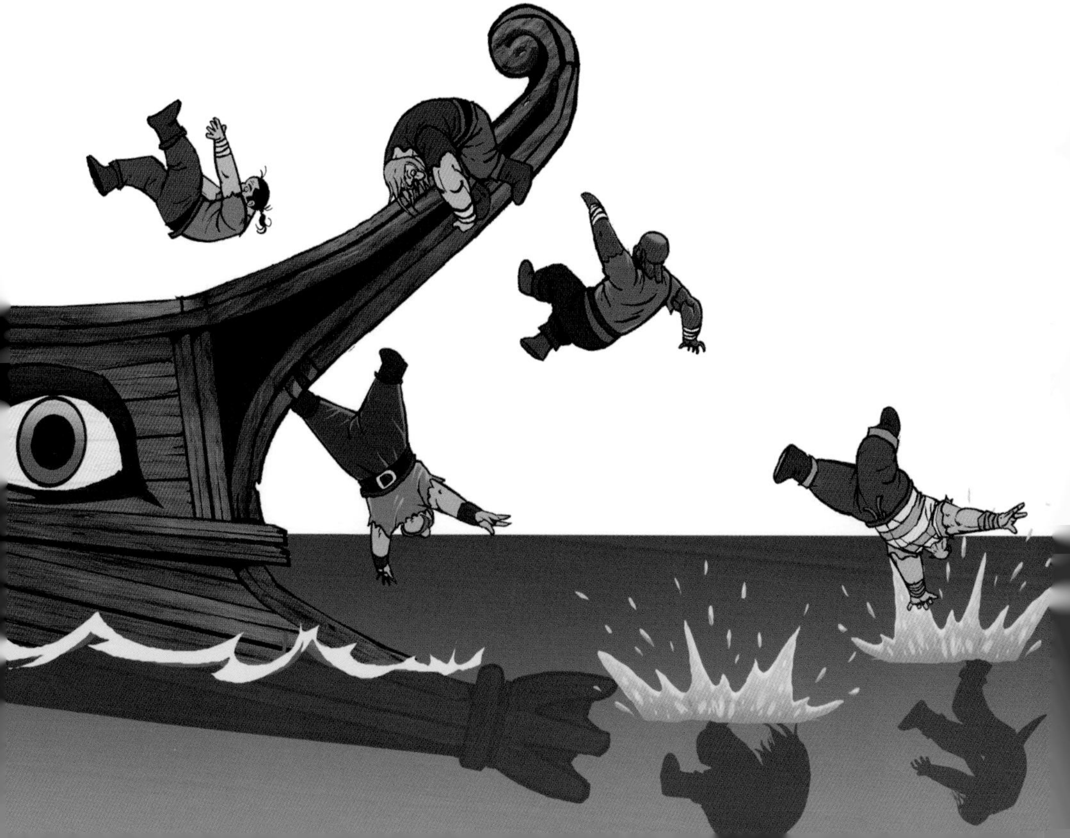

OUCH! OUCH! OUCH!

I grazed my shoulder as I slid along the deck. Shifty, with his lightning reflexes, has gripped a pole with his tongue. He has avoided the worst. Foxy, Musky and Yeti have fallen in a jumble in a corner.

Unfortunately, I discover with horror, what we have hit is not a SANDBAR.

A gigantic tentacle thumps the deck.

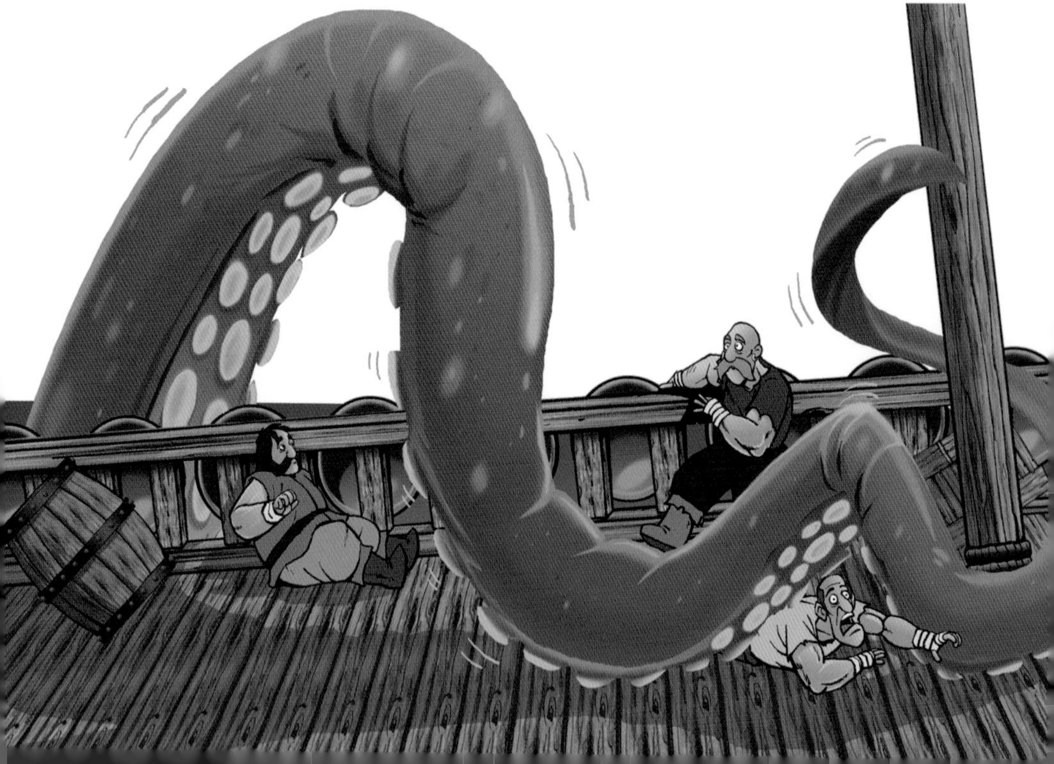

Octopus Aboard!

Yeti can barely contain himself, he is so excited by this monstrous apparition.

"Bring it on! No, really, bring *it* on!"

The weasel doesn't hesitate, or think, before he storms toward the enormous arm.

Billy Stuart called it a tentacle, but, in fact, if this is an octopus, it has eight arms, not tentacles. The main difference is that an arm has suckers down its entire length, whereas a tentacles has suckers only at its end. Tentacles are used for feeding, sensing and grasping, while arms are good for all those things plus have the bonus feature of being able to attach to surfaces and hold the octopus in place while it is resting.

SOMETIMES...OFTEN...ALWAYS, in fact, Yeti's courage is inversely proportional to the size of his fists. He is scared of no one. Didn't he go after the Minotaur on its own turf in the labyrinth? Brave, even though the half-man, half-beast creature never even realized that it had a weasel attached to its ankle.

I watch the following events occur, unable to move to help. The arm **SWEEPS** a part of the deck,

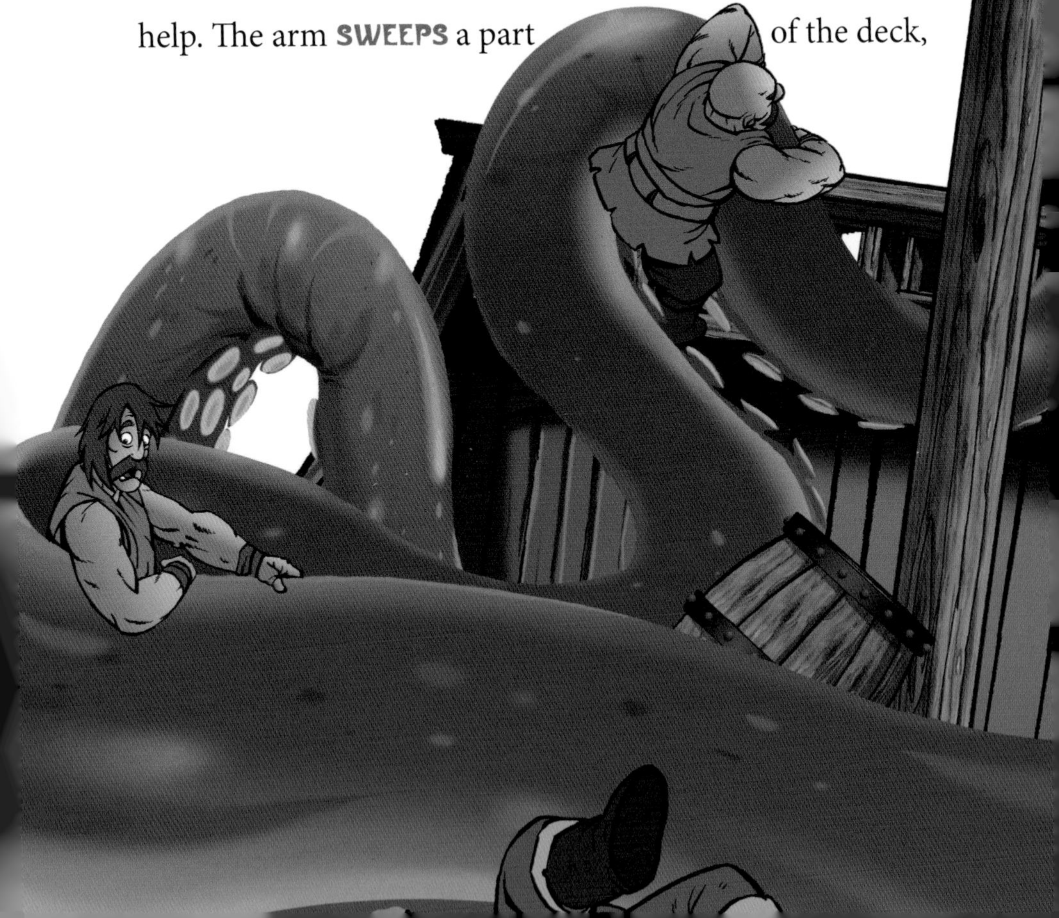

which THROWS three men overboard, KNOCKS OUT four and WOUNDS five. Yeti, due to his agility and size, succeeds in avoiding repeated assaults and manages to climb on top of the arm.

How can he keep his balance? Probably because his legs are so short.

The weasel literally gallops across the arm, which UNDULATES with unpredictable movements. Suddenly it stops moving and presses against the sides of the boat. It's as if the creature wants to hoist itself out of the water.

The **HORROR**! We see the beast in all its ugliness. It is a massive octopus with a gigantic head—it is monstrous! It wraps its other arms around the ship.

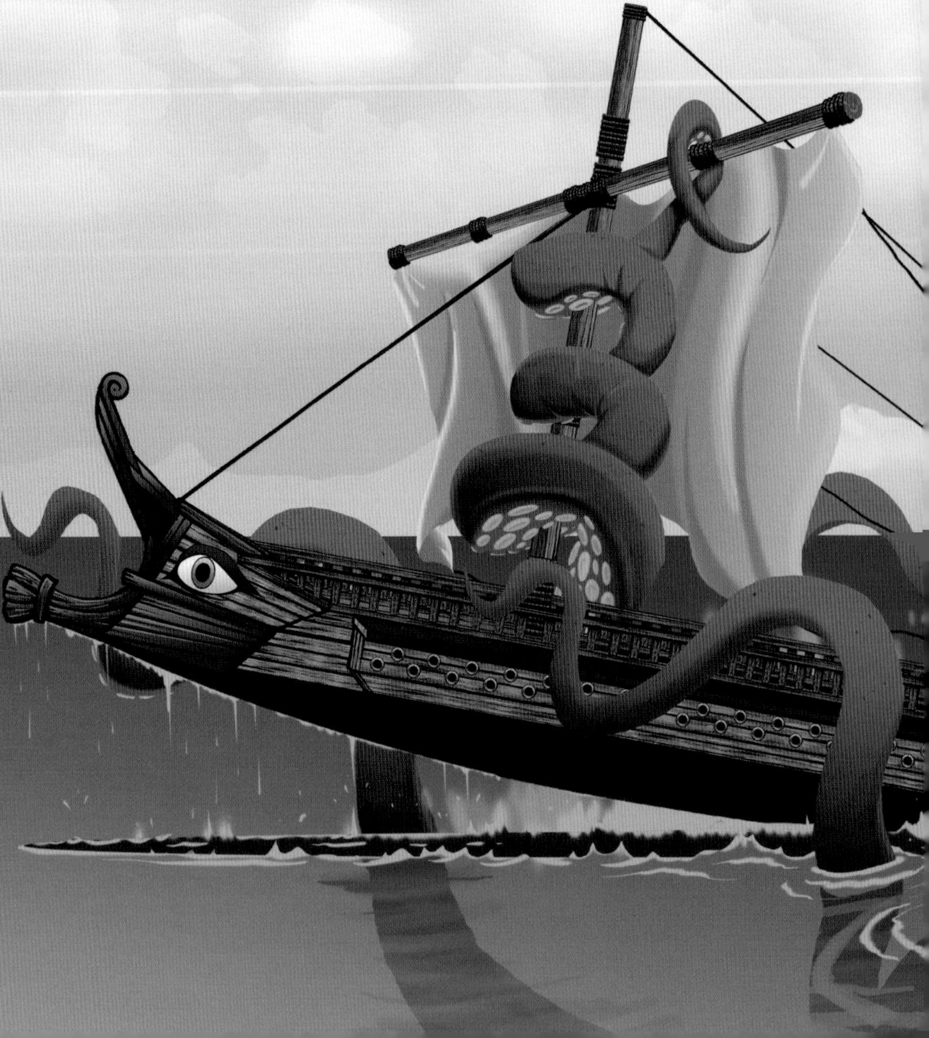

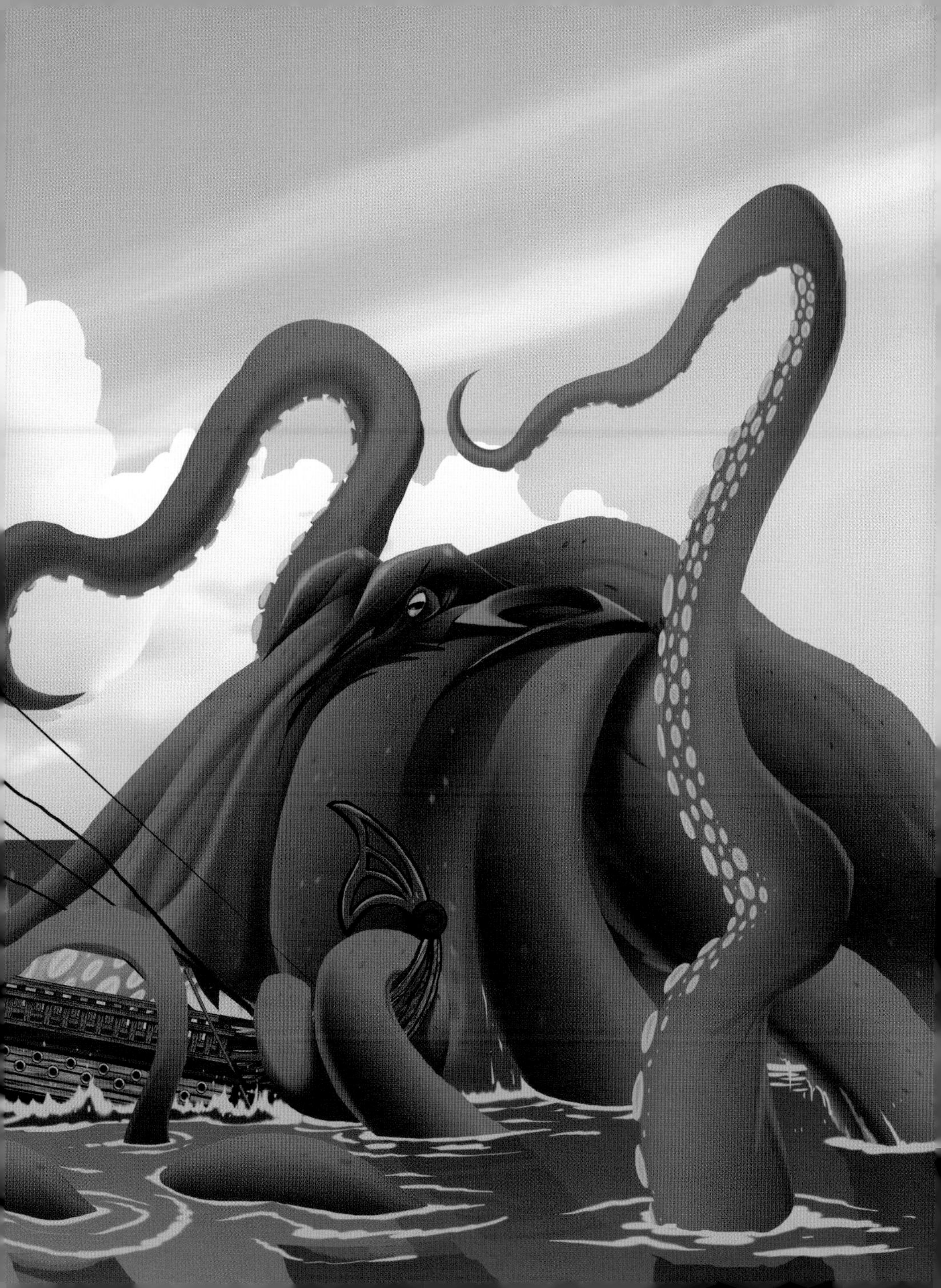

Unless an octopus has had an accident, it has eight arms in total. And spiders have eight legs and eight eyes!

I worry we are about to hear a SINISTER CRACK, a telltale sound of destruction that will see us ending up in the sea.

The bow of the boat has been lifted out of the water by the weight of the massive octopus resting on the stern (the front and back of the boat, in other words). The octopus's eye is so big that the weasel's entire body, from head to toe, is reflected in its giant mirror of an eyeball.

"**TO US!**"

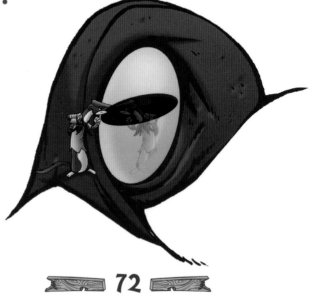

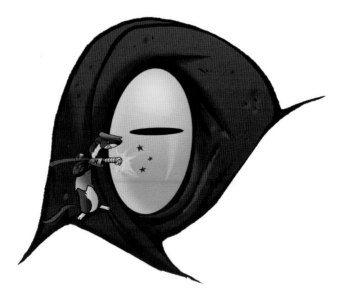

Yeti makes a fist and **BING!** punches the monster right in the eye!

What happens next is unexpected but not unhoped for! The octopus lets the vessel go and pulls back in an effort to see better. Yeti jumps off its head at the last second, avoiding falling into the water. Free from the weight of the beast, the bow of the ship loudly falls back down on the water.

We breathe a sigh of relief.

"TO YOUR PLACES!" shouts the captain.

The weasel is ready for another fight.

"Bring it on! No, really, bring *it* on, squid!"

"Octopus," points out Foxy.

The sailors, now in position and armed, prepare for another attack.

But it doesn't come from the sea.

AAAAAAARRRKKK!

"**KABILLIONS** of crusty-clawed crawfish in that Bulstrode River!"

The roc is back, with two more boulders in his claws.

Things are going from bad to worse!

Brawling Monsters

We are caught between two fires. Which one do we put out first? The roc that's on his way to bomb us with stones? Or the giant octopus that is just taking a break before it tries to sink us again?

We had our arms full with ONE monster, and now there are TWO!

And now I understand how a crawfish must feel when it's stuck between two raccoons…

Yeti doesn't miss a beat.

His eyes go from the octopus to the roc, from the roc to the octopus. He prances around the entire deck of the boat, yelling:

"Bring it on! No, really, bring *it* on! Which one of you wants it first?"

It seems that neither one is interested in a fight, so Yeti snaps his fingers and addresses a sailor.

"**HEY!** You there! Go big or go home! Come fight me!"

Musky manages to bring him back to us.

So will we be crushed or drowned? Or both? Which of those deaths is the least painful?

AAAAAAAAAAAAARRRK!

The roc throws the first stone and, luckily, misses.

SPLASH!

The projectile almost hits the octopus, which throws up two arms in protest.

What is wrong with you? it seems to be saying.

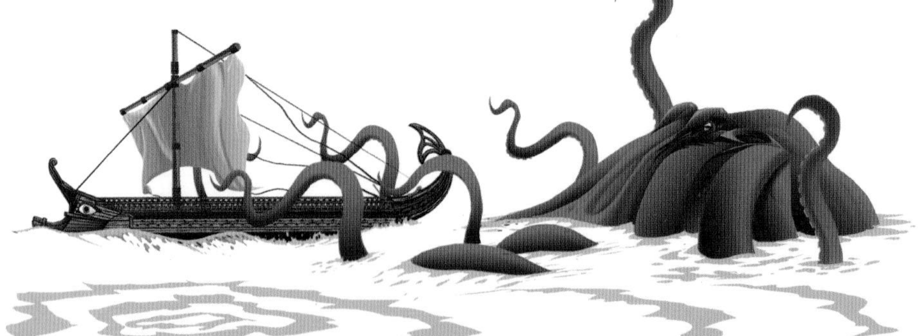

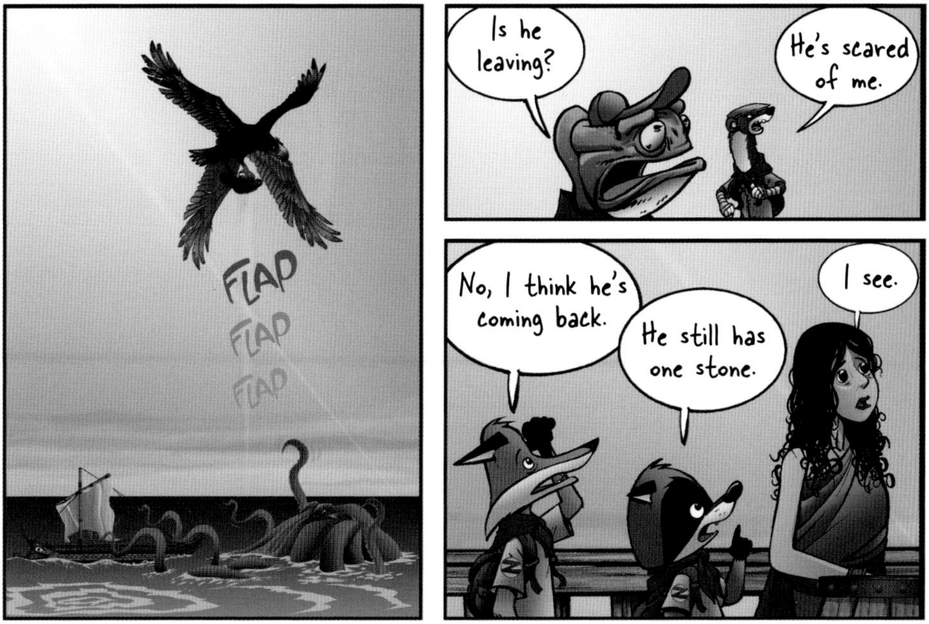
FLAP
FLAP
FLAP
Is he leaving?
He's scared of me.
No, I think he's coming back.
He still has one stone.
I see.

The Zintrepids study the bird's flight pattern. The octopus also watches the feathered giant.

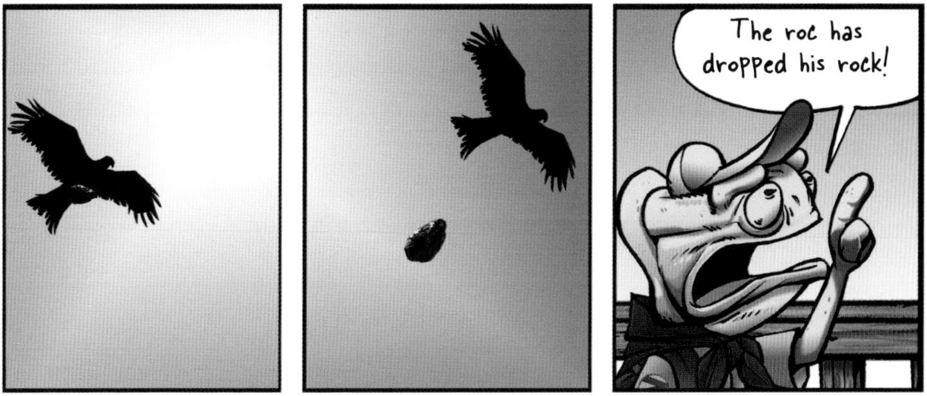
The roc has dropped his rock!

In just a few seconds, the boulder will hit our boat and finish us, and the beasts will fight over our carcasses.

There is a whistle, some frightened cries, and an astonishing…

SPLAT!

Not *splash!* Nor *craaaaaack!*

SPLAT!

Followed by an **AAAAAAAAAAAARRRRRK!**

The bird cries out in triumph.He has hit his target! But it wasn't the ship—it was the octopus! The boulder landed right in its face!

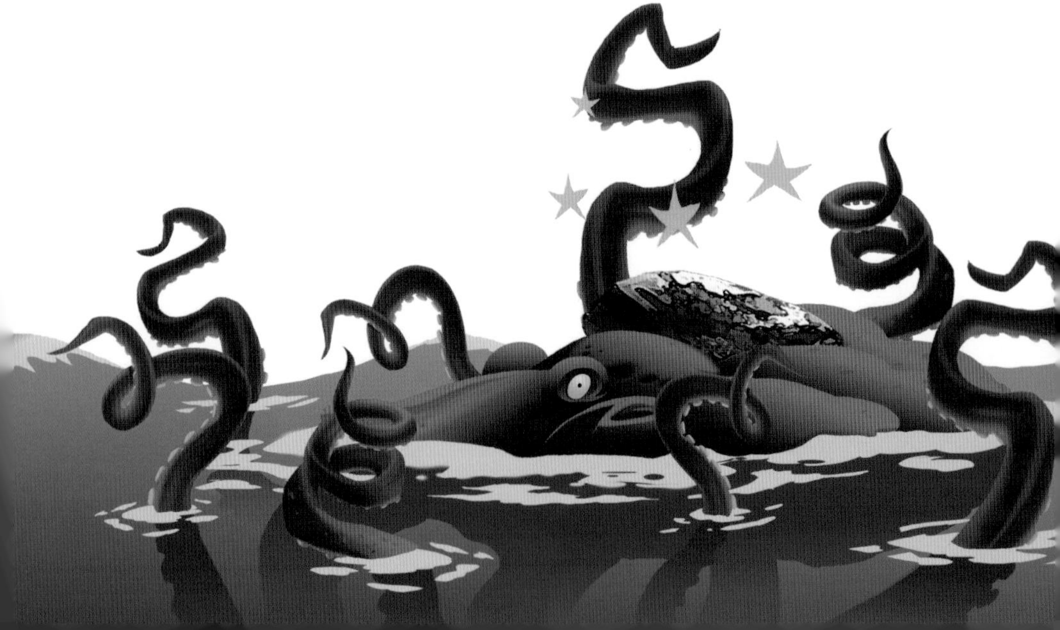

Is the octopus dead? I believe so. It lies completely still, floating on the water. I don't think anyone could survive such an impact.

The bird, claws out, dives with **LIGHTNING SPEED** toward his prey. When he gets to the octopus, he picks it up and flies away as if it isn't any heavier than a simple **SHEEP**.

"I hope he likes seafood," says Shifty.

"We have to follow him!" orders the captain.

There is no danger of losing sight of them because of the sheer size of both the roc and the octopus, whose arms are dangling down. But the arms aren't limp…they're moving! The octopus is JIGGLING, trying to escape from the roc. To the bird's dismay, the boulder has only stunned the beast.

The arms grab the roc's wings and pull them down. Unable to fly, the roc falls toward the sea. The two beasts are entwined in a strange, devilish ballet.

SPLASH!

The roc tries furiously to escape the octopus's arms. Who will triumph in this clash of titans?

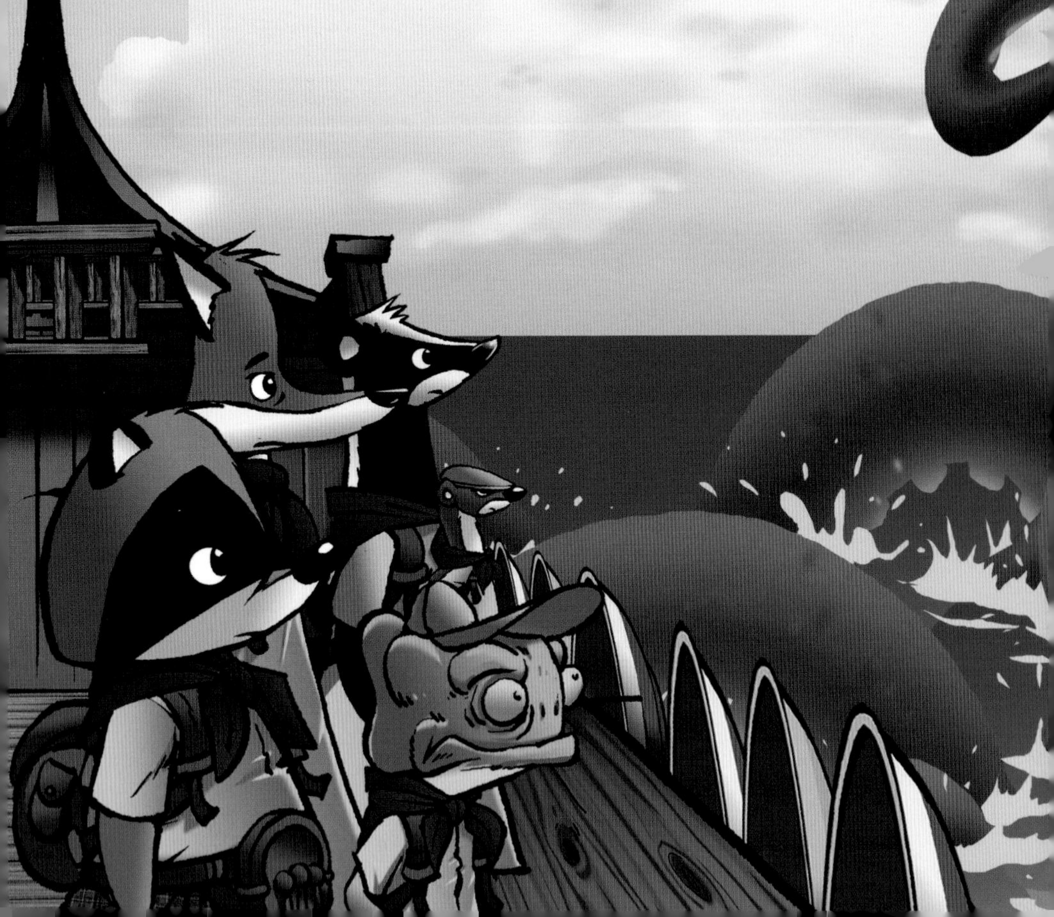

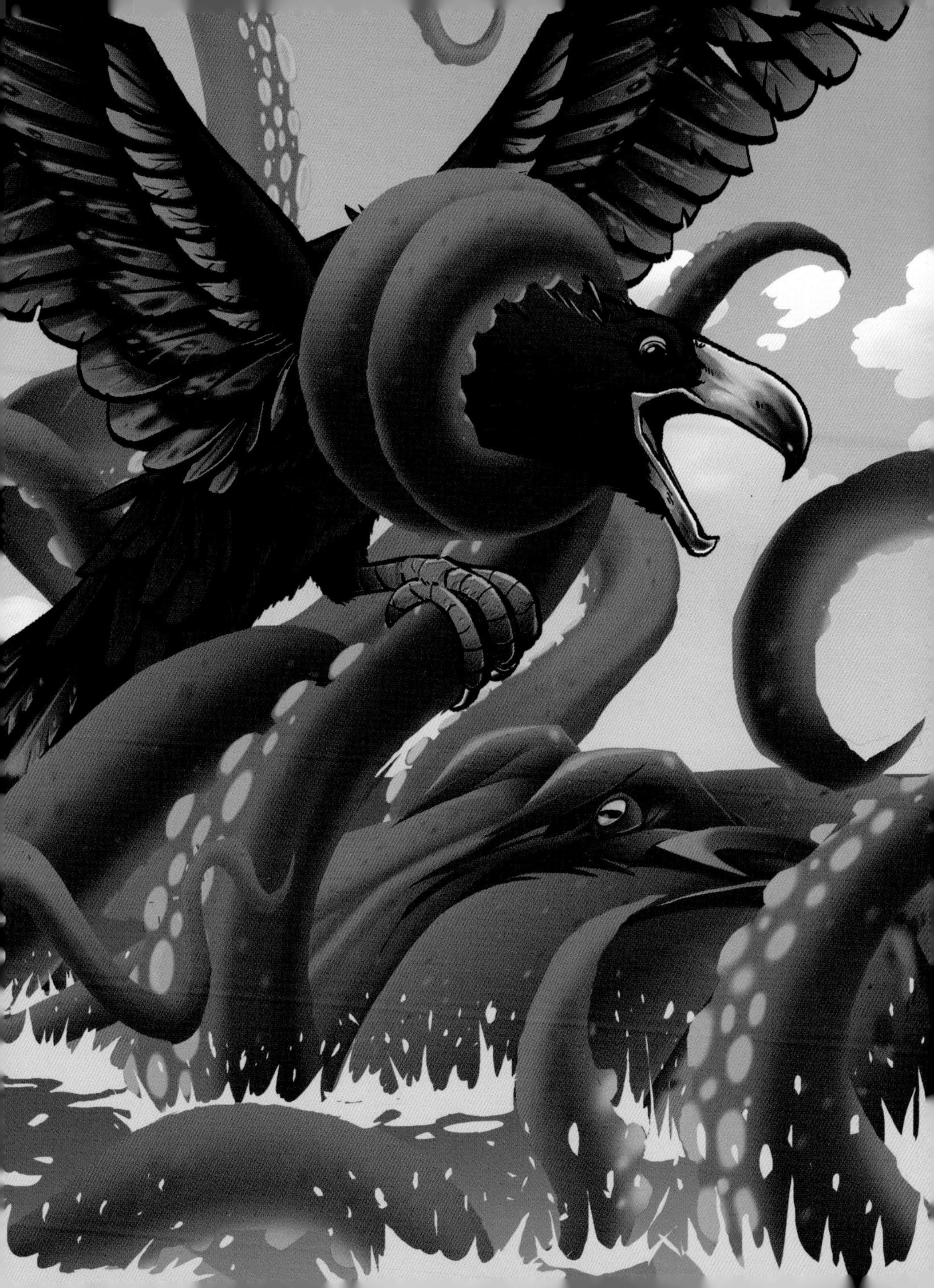

"It's no longer our PROBLEM," says the captain, maneuvering the boat away from the fight.

Foxy isn't listening to Loslobos. She takes a spear and throws it with all her might at the octopus. The octopus, getting it in the side of the HEAD, releases its grip, and the bird takes his chance to flee.

As the roc flies away, he looks back and gives Foxy a grateful look.

AAAAAAAAAAARRRK!

"My pleasure!" she replies.

Yeti sulks, his arms across his chest.

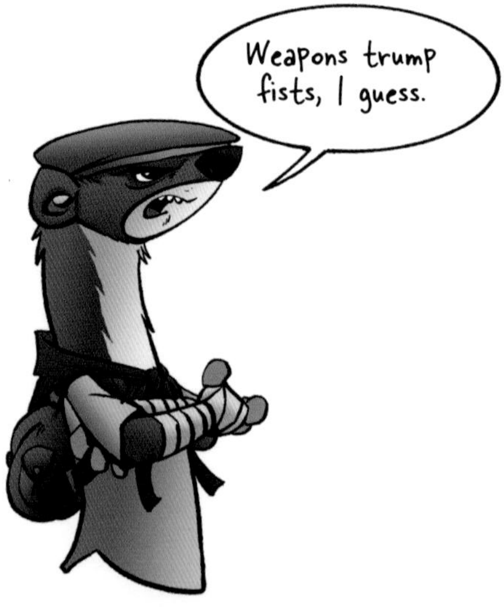
Weapons trump fists, I guess.

Land!

"Kabillions of crusty-clawed crawfish in that Bulstrode River!"

"**LAND!** An island! Straight ahead!"

The sailors shout with joy. It's time to celebrate! They leap into each other's arms, they sing, they dance. Someone drags Musky into a crazy twirl. Stunned, the skunk sprays!

SSHHHHHH!

Right onto her poor partner, whose face goes from **RED** to **GRAY** to seasick **GREEN**. Grimacing, he runs to the gunwale and throws up his dinner into the sea.

The celebrations are short-lived, because the sea starts to churn as we approach the island. Right now the captain has to find somewhere we can dock.

Unfortunately, this bit of forgotten land has no easy access. Loslobos realizes that the only solution is a bay toward the west. To get there, he'll have to avoid several underwater REEFS.

"We don't have a choice," Loslobos says to his crew. "Everyone to their posts!"

A sailor perched on the front of the ship yells:

"Dolphins!"

The sea suddenly calms, and an entrance to the bay becomes accessible. Now it seems possible to find a path through the reefs without getting in too much trouble. A pod of dolphins swims alongside us.

A sailor bursts out laughing, pointing at the water ahead.

"Strange! The dolphins are waving at us!"

Intrigued, I get closer, followed by the rest of Zintrepids. In front of my eyes, dozens of dolphins are waving their tails, the tops of their bodies underwater. The scene is spectacular and curious…and just a little bit troubling.

I notice that the dolphins' tails are covered in scales. But if I remember correctly, dolphin skin is smooth, not scaly like fishes'. If only we could see what their heads look like.

Froufrou **BOUNDS** into Foxy's arms and starts barking. **WOOF! WOOF! WOOF!**

The dolphins plunge down into the water, their tails leaving a wake.

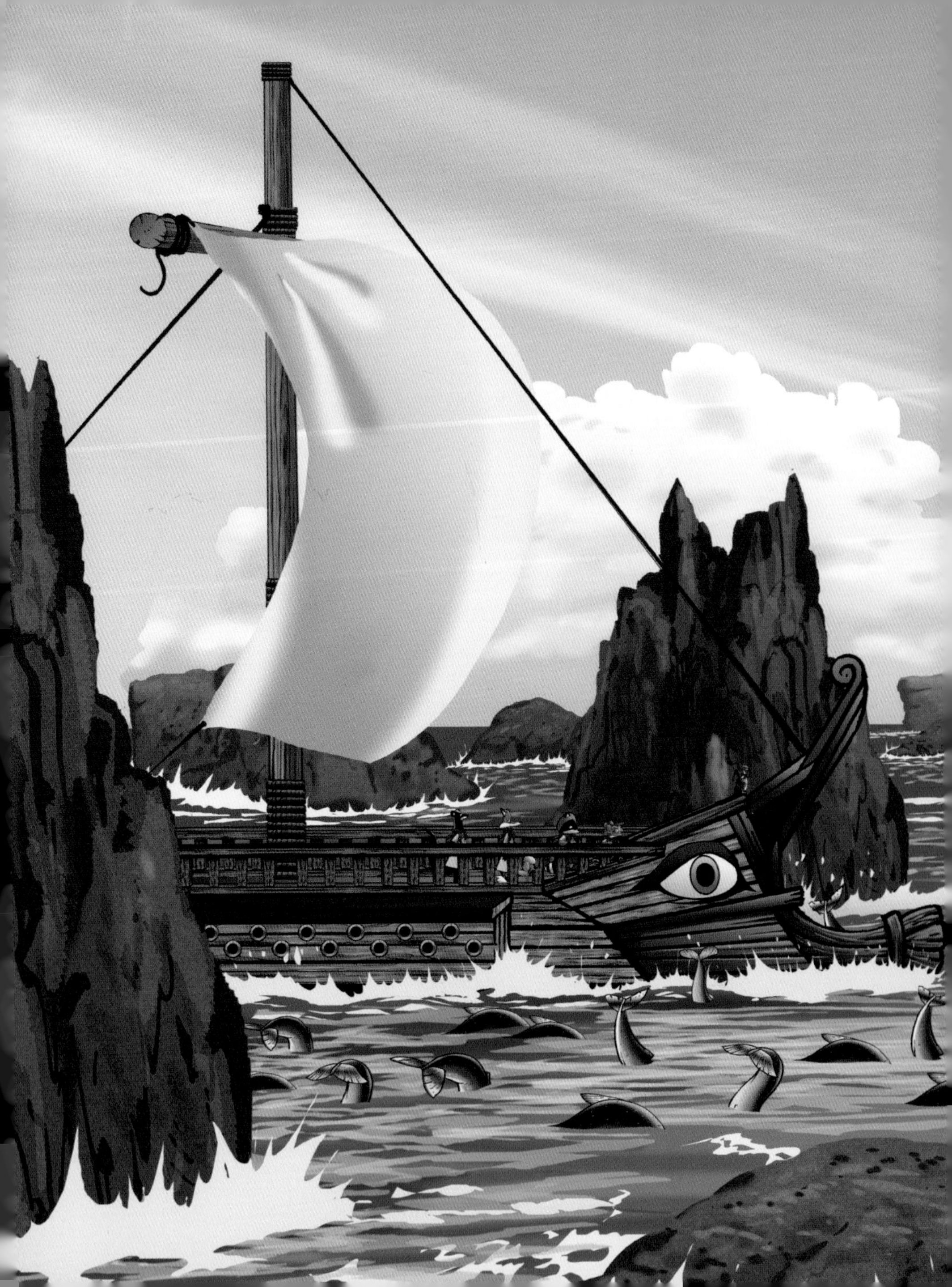

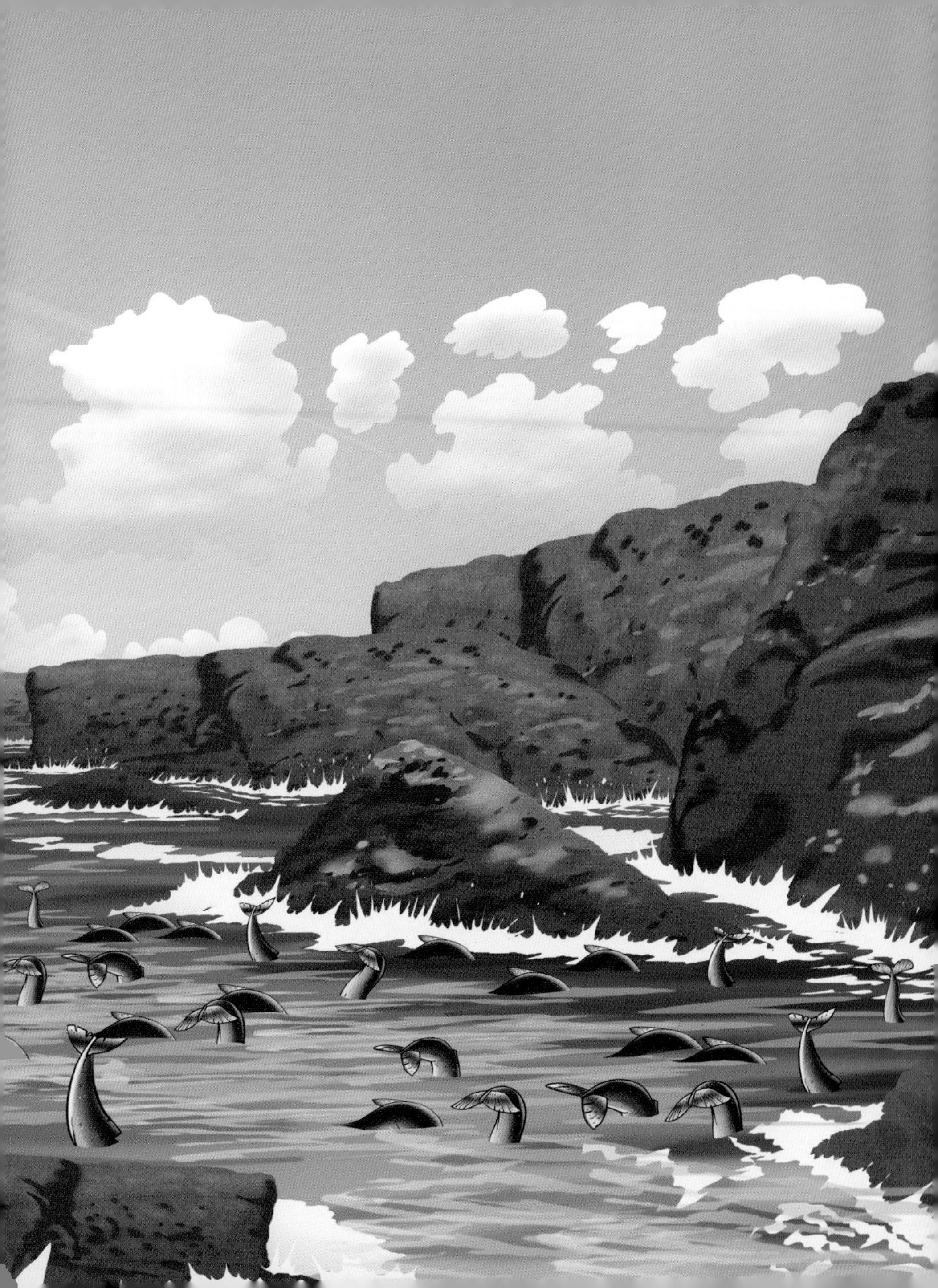

"**GREAT**, dog!" I say, annoyed. "You scared the poor dolphins away. They only wanted to guide us to land."

But FrouFrou trembles with joy, simply happy that I am speaking to him.

"What is that?" asks a sailor who sounds very worried.

Interesting.

The creatures have come back to the surface to help us out. But they're not dolphins, they're...

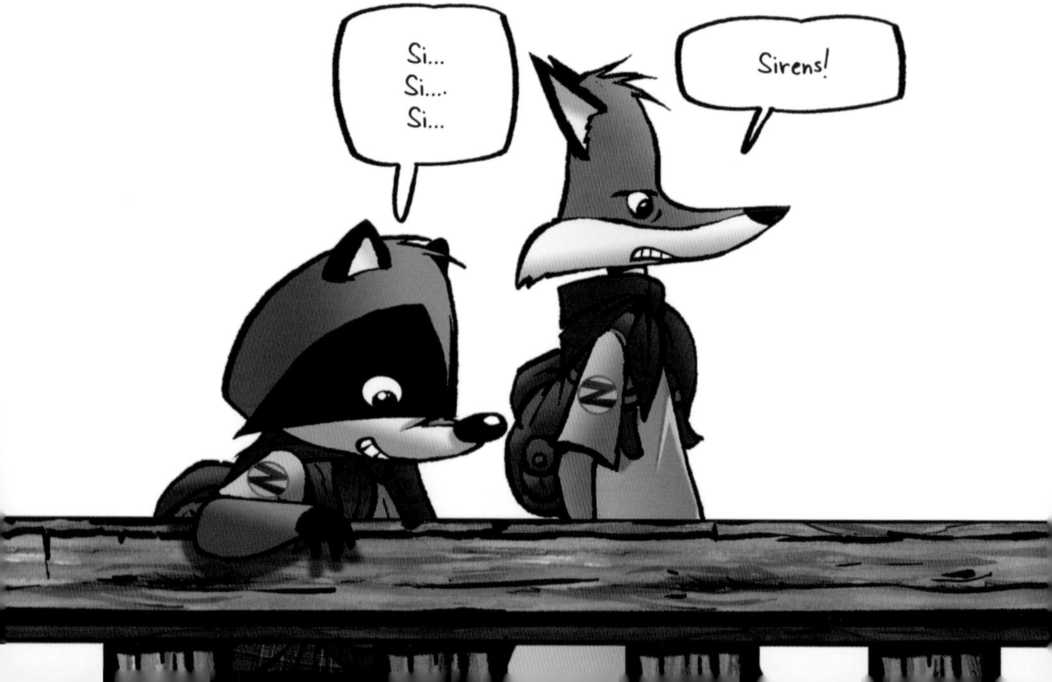
Si...
Si....
Si...
Sirens!

Chapter 13

The Sirens' Song

Everyone leaves their posts to come see these half-women, half-fish creatures. I'm curious. Do they want to lead us safely to the island?

Yeti seems **HYPNOTIZED**. Under his breath he starts muttering, "Bring it on. No, really, bring *it* on." But without his usual gusto.

Having fallen completely under the sirens' **SPELL**, a sailor jumps into the water to join them. Several sirens encircle him. One of them, with pale skin and long dark hair, strokes his cheek.

She offers him her hand and separates him from the group while the rest of the sirens stifle their smirks.

Not at all enchanted, Foxy murmurs, "This isn't normal."

"Are you jealous?" Shifty asks.

The sailor in the water is struggling to keep swimming, and the siren is supporting him. She holds his hand firmly as she plunges underwater.

I hold my breath! **FIVE** seconds. **TEN** seconds. **FIFTEEN** seconds.

The sailor still hasn't come up. I fear the worst with each second that passes.

"Breathe, Billy Stuart!" Musky says.

I didn't realize I had stopped breathing. I wondered why I was starting to feel dizzy.

The sailor never resurfaces, but the siren with the dark hair does…and she has the look of someone who's completed her task.

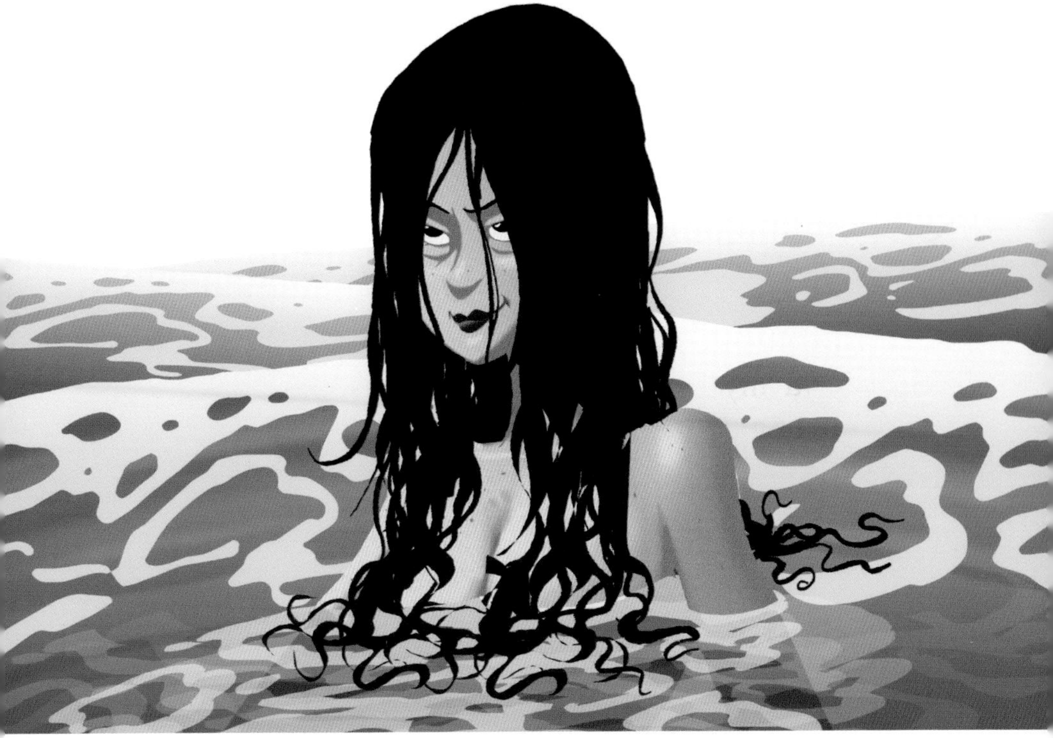

It's a trap. The sirens' intentions are as CLEAR as the seawater. They want to drown the ship's crew. If we stay on board, we'll be safe, because they can't leap out of the water.

The rest of the crew is HORRIFIED by what has happened to their companion, and they take up arms. They must defend themselves and chase the sirens away.

The other sirens silently surround the one with the dark hair, who appears to be their leader. And then, without as much as a word, they move in unison to surround the boat. How do they communicate with each other without speaking? Is it telepathy?

Telepathy is a way to communicate without using words, relying just on your thoughts.

The sirens open their mouths and start to make strange noises. I can hear some **mmmmmmmms** and some eeeeeeeees. Some oooooooooohs and some **aaaaaaahs**. Lots of vowels and very few consonants.

Their sweet song invades the ship and the sailors' souls. All they can hear is the sirens' call. They are under the spell, hypnotized.

I realize it's not really a song but an invitation.

An invitation to join them.

Because just then another sailor jumps into the water.

And now it's too late for him.

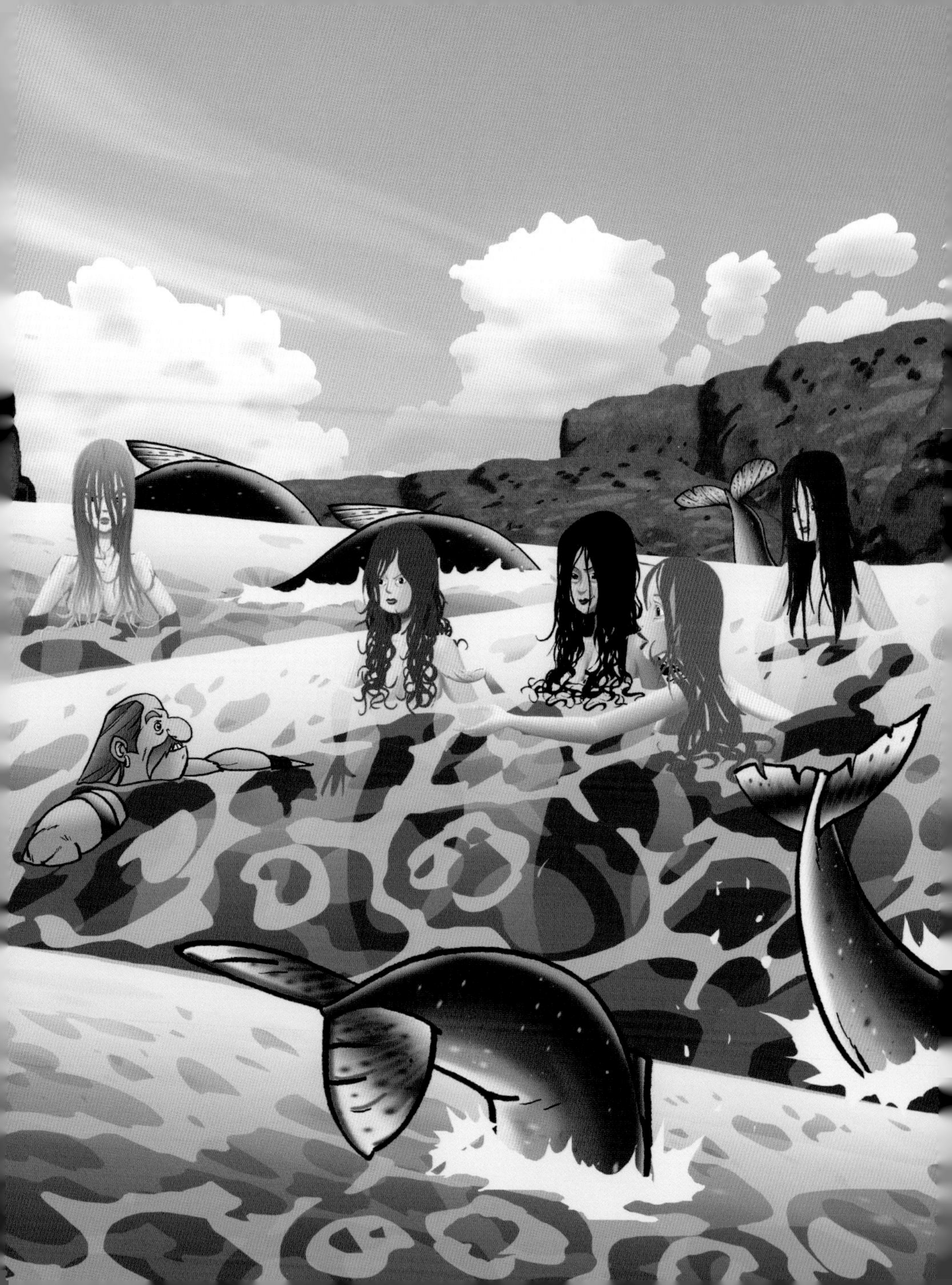

ANAGRAMS

By changing the order of the letters in a word, you can create a new word. For example, *calm* can also spell *clam*. Change the order of the letters in each word in **bold** to make a brand-new one.

One of these dangerous ladies **rinses** her hair in the waves. Then she joins her sisters as they enchant the sailors with their songs.

When your shipmates want to sacrifice you in wild **parties**, they have become dangerous mutineers.

As the ships and crew **bake** in the sun, the roc appears and drops a boulder from its sharp pointy mouth.

Is it safe for Billy and the Zintrepids to sail near the giant octopus's **garden**?

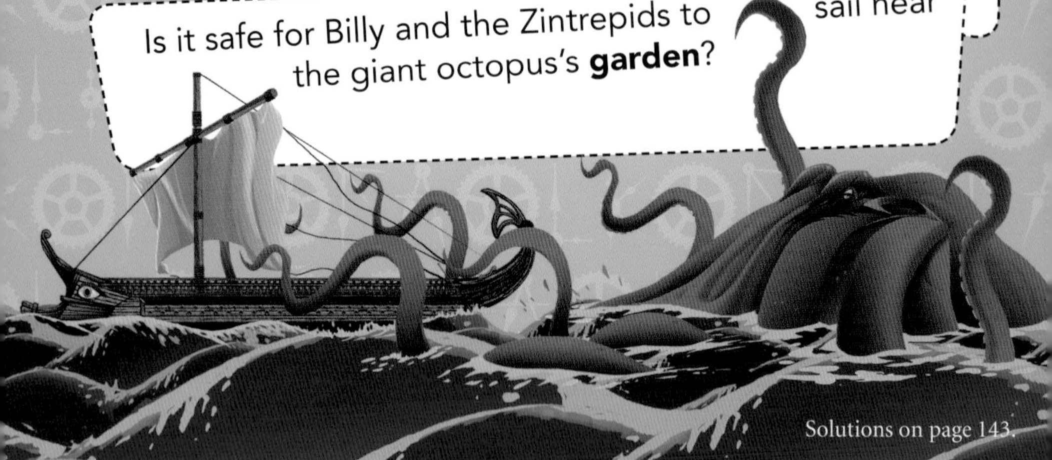

Solutions on page 143.

The Cry

As I already said, the sirens' call invaded the ship and enchanted the sailors. But not the Zintrepids, and not Timoree, the captain's sister.

We only witness the horrible spell that affects all the men onboard. Each **SPLASH** indicates another sailor has jumped overboard.

The sirens' song continues to weave a trap around the crew.

But suddenly FrouFrou howls.

AAOOoooooooOYUUUUuu!

The sirens go quiet for a moment, then start their song again.

The dog's howl has had only a brief effect on the creatures.

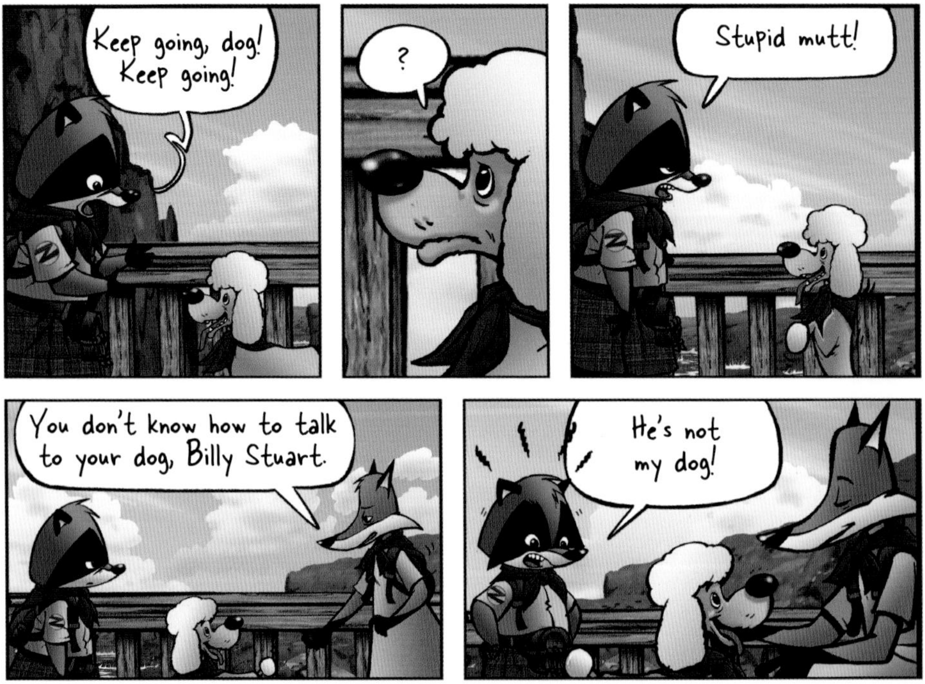
Keep going, dog! Keep going!
?
Stupid mutt!
You don't know how to talk to your dog, Billy Stuart.
He's not my dog!

The fox comes over to the poodle. Behind us, Loslobos is seized with spasms, and Timoree struggles to cover her brother's ears to keep him safe.

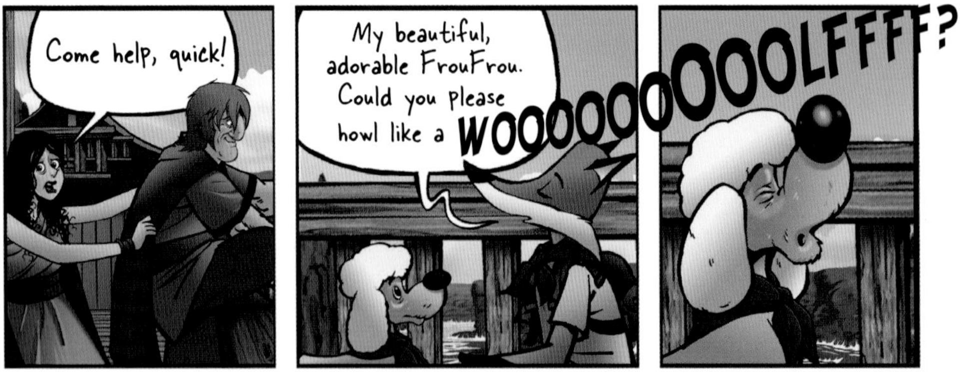
Come help, quick!
My beautiful, adorable FrouFrou. Could you please howl like a
WOOOOOOOOOLFFFF?

The reaction is immediate. The sirens stop singing and the sailors come out of their hypnotized state.

AOOOOOOOOOOOOUUUU!
"C'mon, everybody, we need to scream!"

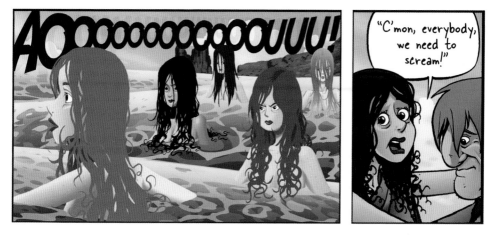

With the Zintrepids all howling, the crew joins in. The sailors understand the **URGENCY** of the situation.

And it works! The sirens are chased away by the noise!

Repeat after me: six sirens stopping singing serenely save themselves super slippery-ly.
Say it six times with salty sweets in your mouth.

WHO AM I?

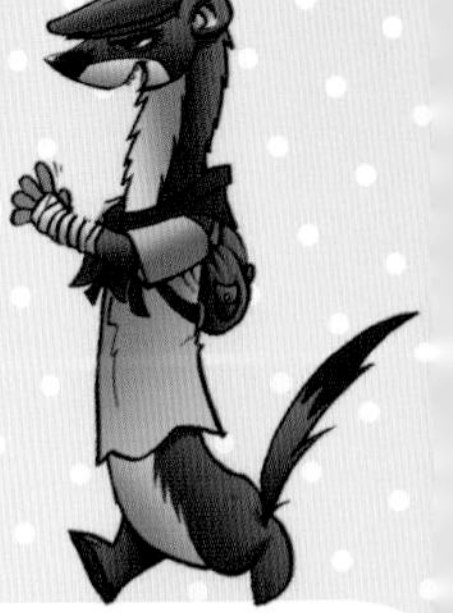

Who am I?

I advance by retreating, and Billy Stuart lets nothing get in the way of picking me up.

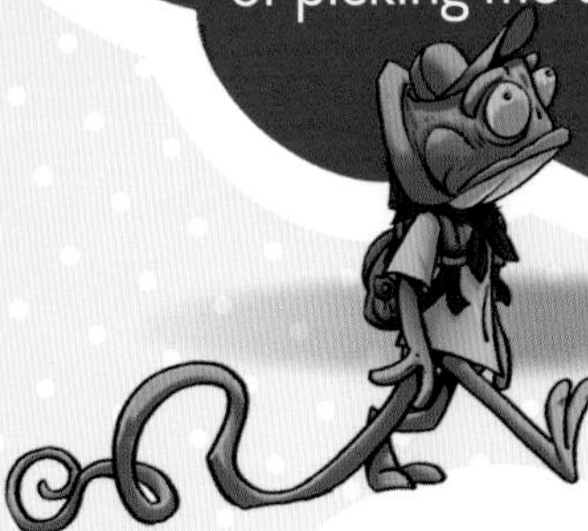

Who am I?

I've toured the world, all the while staying in one corner.

Who am I?

I am the color that Shifty, the chameleon, sees when he looks in the mirror.

Solution on page 143.

On the Beach

Once they are out of danger, the crew still onboard starts fishing sailors out of the sea. Some of the men had a close brush with death—they got within an arm's reach of being DEVOURED by the sirens.

Having come back to his senses, Loslobos thanks his sister and the Zintrepids for pulling his crew from the sirens' claws.

"It's our sweetie-pie FrouFrou that we have to thank, Captain," Foxy says.

She congratulates the dog and showers him with nauseating declarations of love.

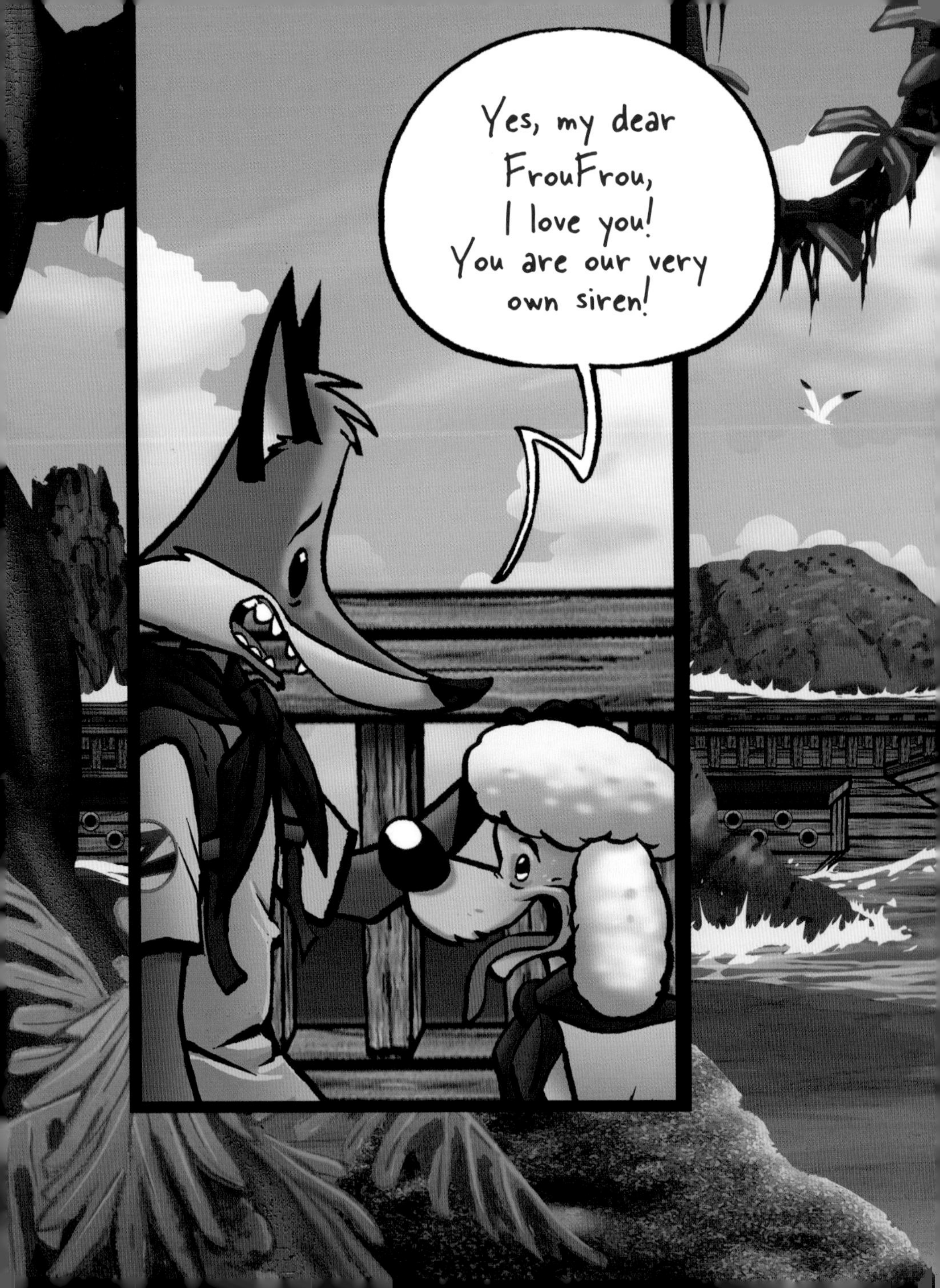
Yes, my dear FrouFrou, I love you! You are our very own siren!

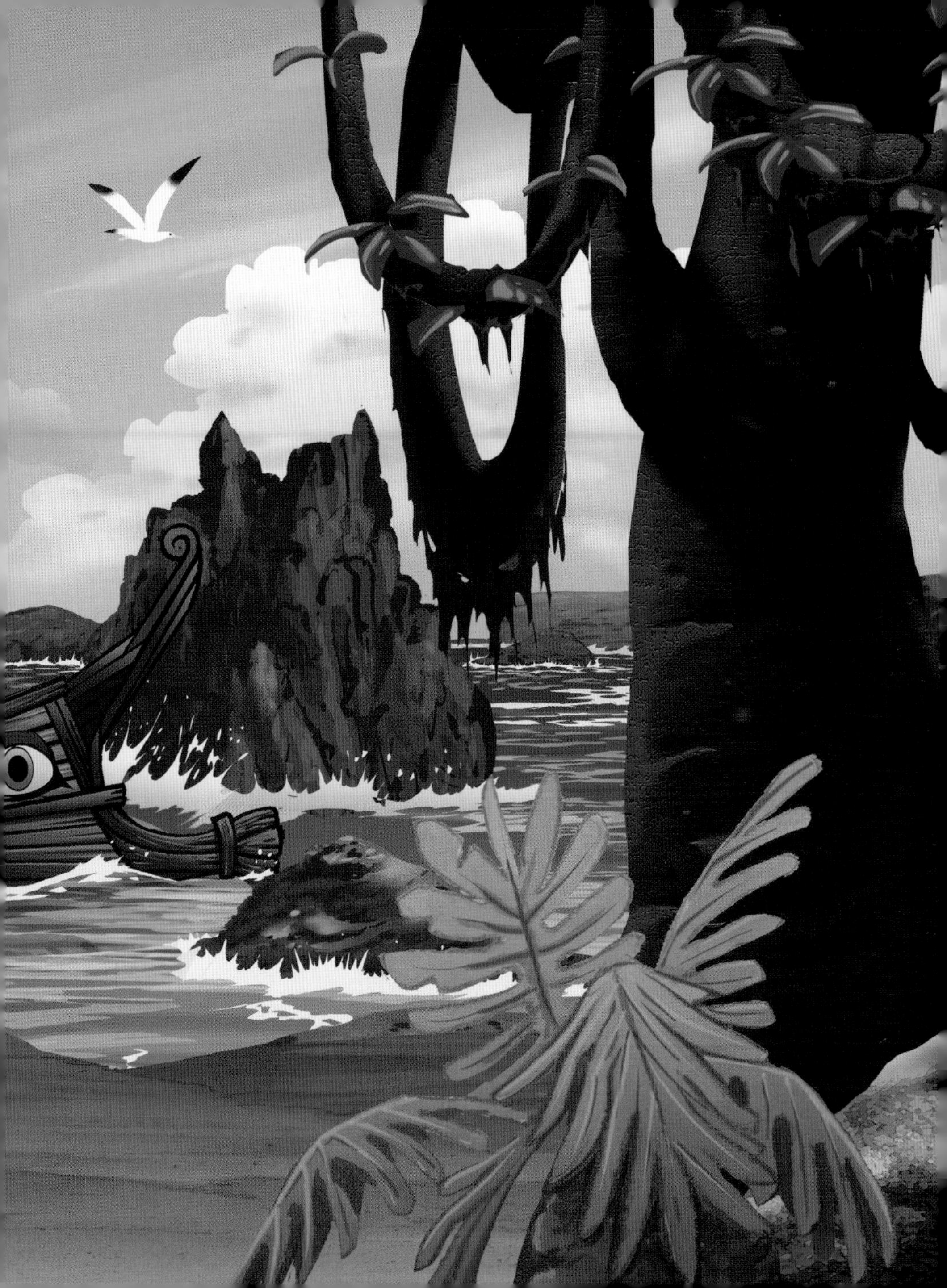

Loslobos expertly steers the ship to shore, managing to avoid the dangerous reefs in our path. The crew cries out in **JOY** as soon as the ship docks, and everyone disembarks as soon as is possible—even Ugobos, to whom the captain has temporarily granted freedom. Quite a few sailors hug the sand, they are so happy to be on dry land.

Night begins to fall. We discover a vast stretch of beach, bordered by **luxurious** jungle. With the sun setting, it is a picture worthy of a postcard.

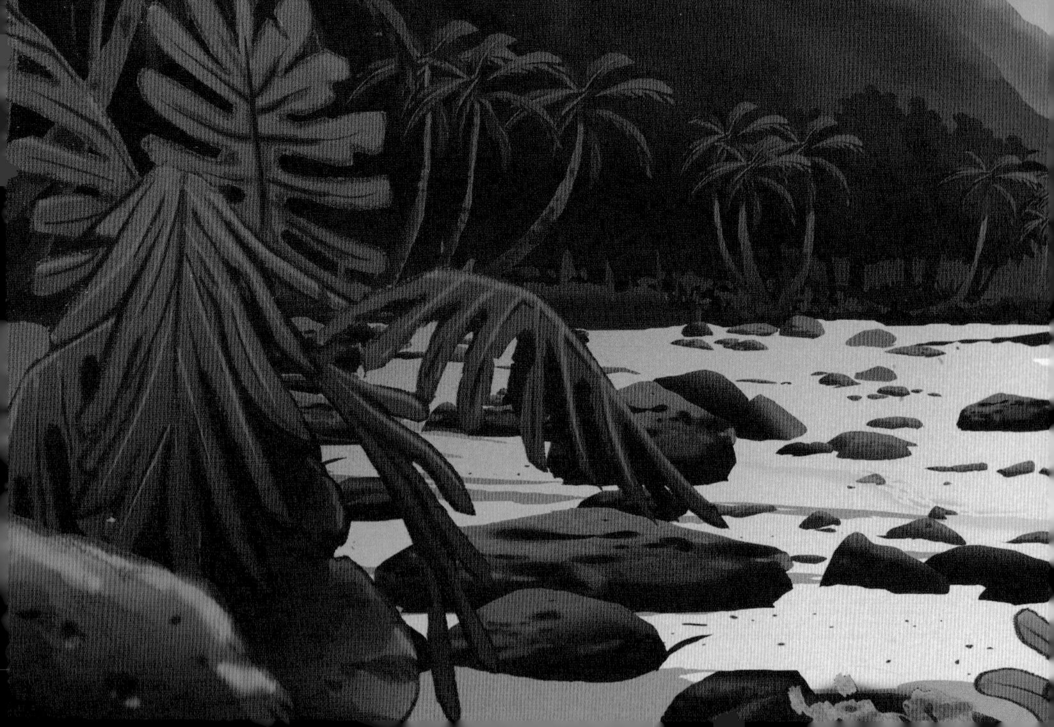

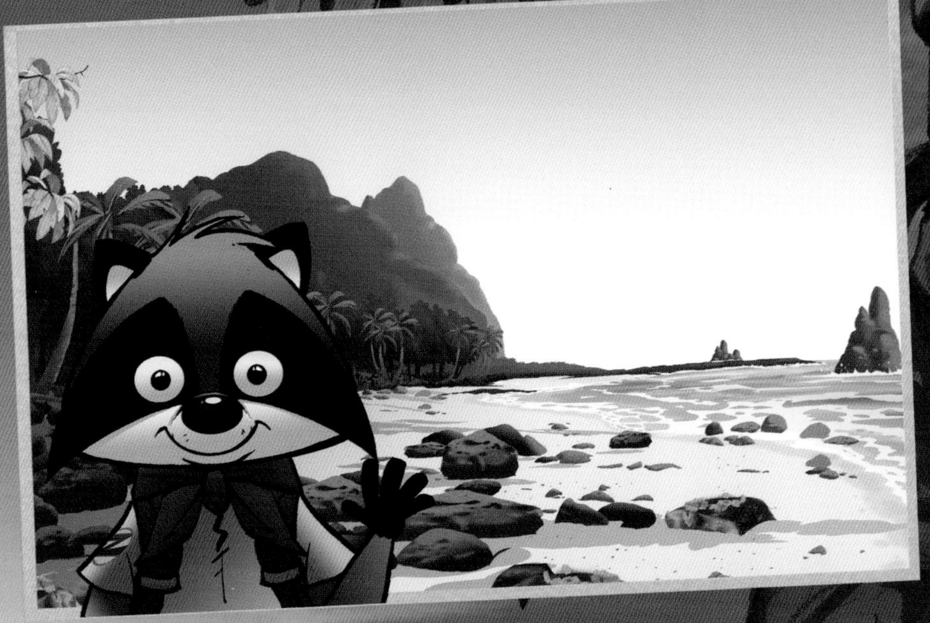

carte postale

Dear Parents

How are you? It's been several centuries since I last wrote. (FYI that's a little time-traveler joke!)

It's very pretty here—and hot, about 30 degrees.

In the heat of the day you have to rest in the shade, otherwise you couldn't stand it.

Speaking of intolerable, you can tell the MacTerrings that their dog, FrouFrou, is still alive—for now. I continue the journey with my friends, the Zintrepids. Until next time.

Your son
Billy Stuart

PS. Dad, if I were you, I wouldn't wait for me to get back to mow the grass. It might get too long.

"We are on a desert island," Musky says.

"It's not deserted now that we're here," Shifty points out.

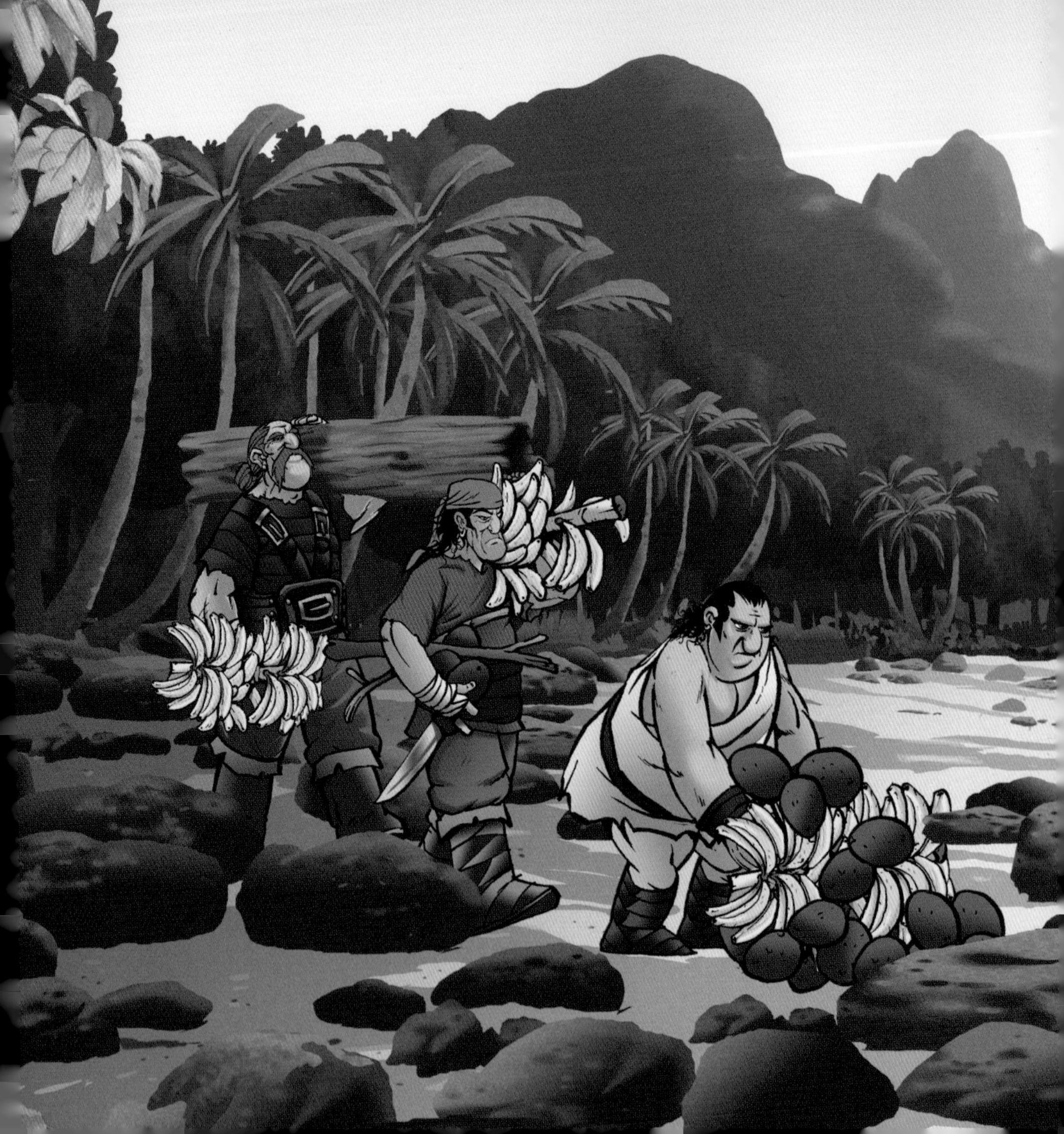

The captain announces that we will explore the island the next morning at sunrise but that now it's time to build a makeshift camp to spend the NIGHT in.

Some men, including Ugobos, are sent to go look for food. With FLAMING torches, they trek deep into the jungle, reappearing shortly thereafter with their arms full of BANANAS and coconuts.

"BY CHANCE, did you see a river with crawfish?"

"Be happy with what you have, Billy Stuart," Foxy says, noticing my disappointment.

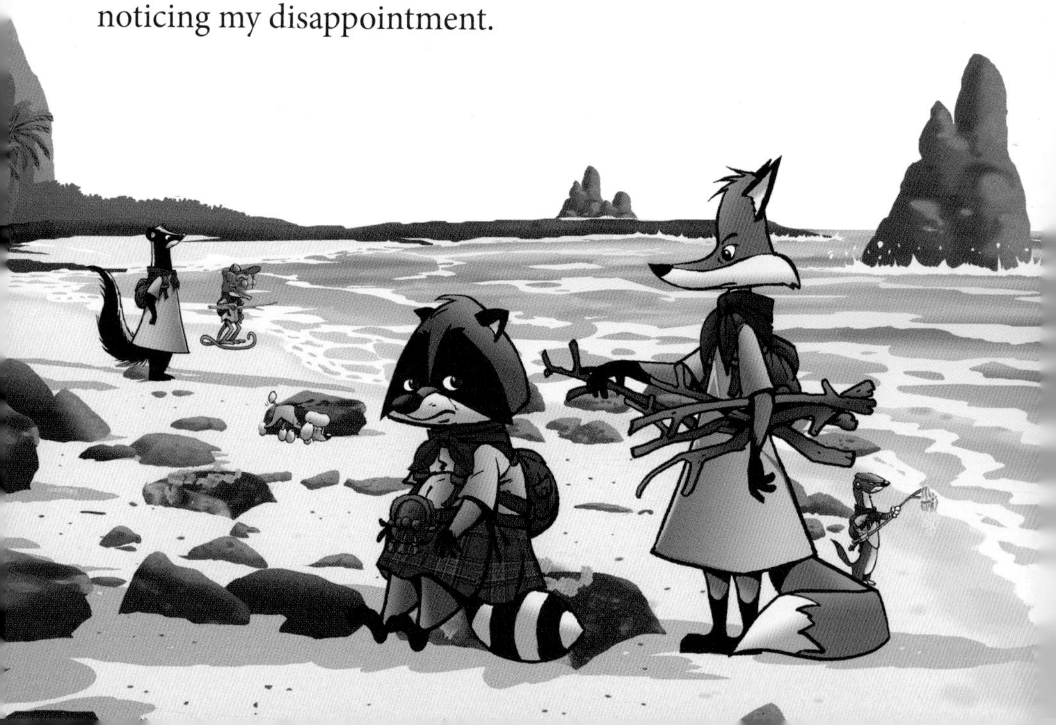

We all gather PIECES OF WOOD to make a fire. Are there wild animals on the island that could attack us in the night? Or will the sirens come back to try to enchant us again?

Like he's heard my thoughts, the captain designates two of his men to stand guard throughout the night.

I'm anxious about sleeping on the beach. I have very sensitive skin, and I'm worried about SAND FLEAS. Once, on a family trip to Virginia, I stretched out on the sand at the beach to rest and was woken up by the tickles of sand fleas. I could see them swarming in my fur. It was AwfUL!

The exact same thing happened to one of my brothers-in-law. He's hairy, like a monkey, and made the poor choice to sleep on the sand. Just like Billy Stuart, he woke up to find his chest swarming with sand fleas. Ever since then, he shaves off all his body hair!

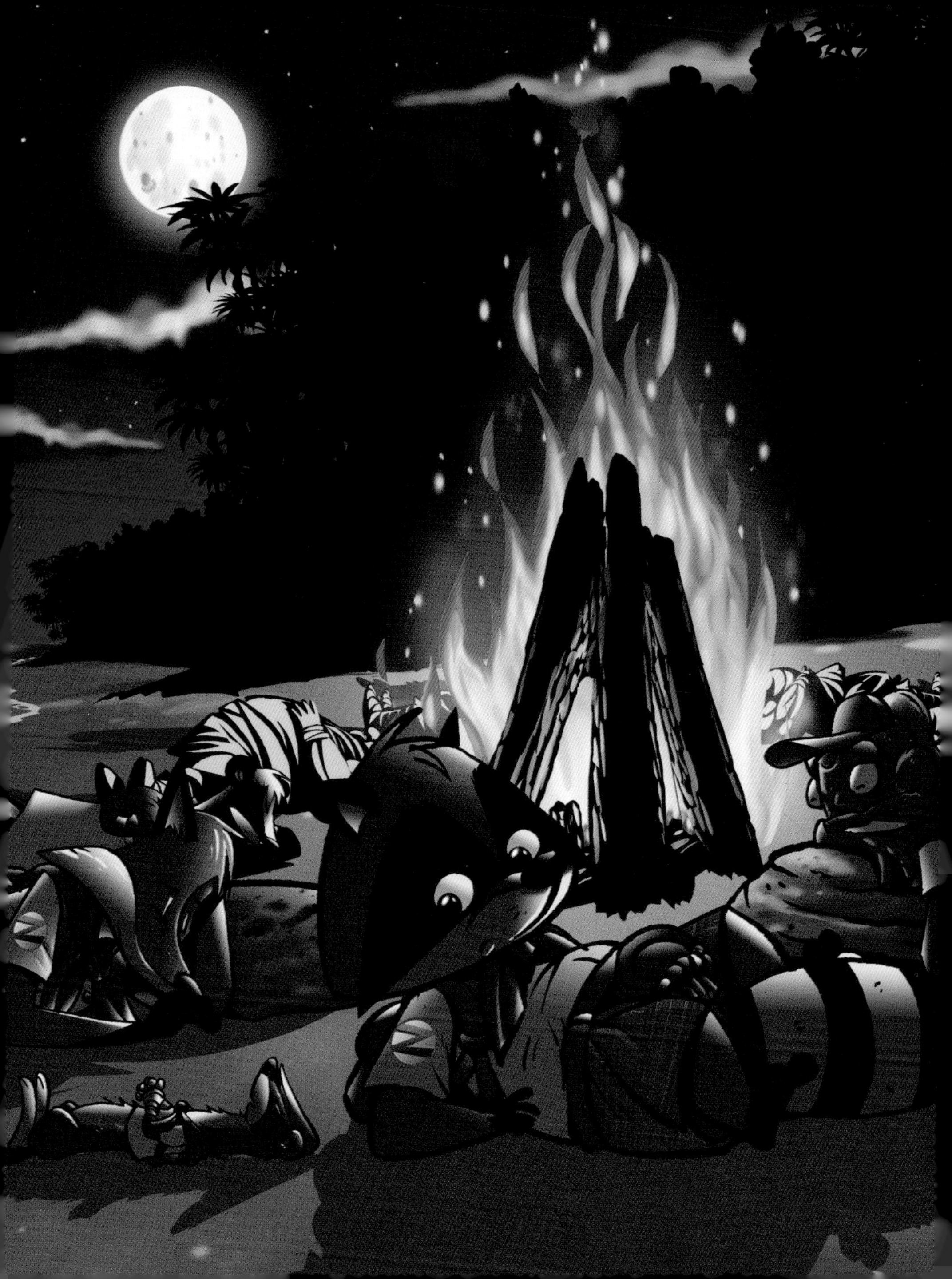

The fatigue and nervous tension of the last few days catches up with me, and my eyelids get heavy. Resistance is futile. My friends sleep deeply. The poodle snores like an airplane engine, and I am the only one bothered by it.

Good night!

CLICKETY CLICKETY

What's that noise?

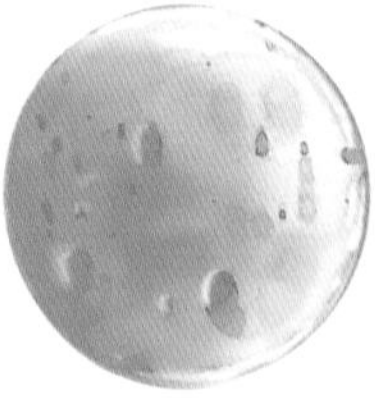

CLICKETY CLICKETY

I jolt upright, my senses on high alert.

CLICKETY CLICKETY

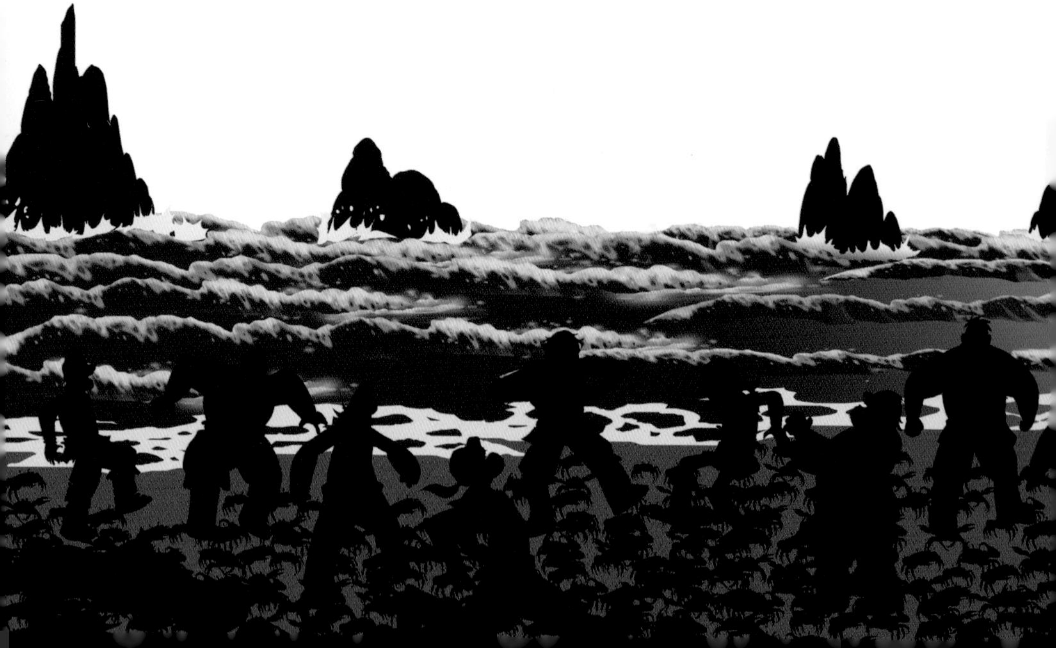

Something moves not far from us. I shake the Zintrepids one after another to wake them up.

"What? Is it already morning, Billy Stuart?" moans Shifty.

"It's the MOON in the sky, Billy Stuart, not the sun," mutters Musky.

CLICKETY CLICKETY CLICKETY

The "clicketies" are multiplying.

Men cry out in the night. No one is asleep anymore. The Zintrepids huddle together. The whole beach seems to be wiggling in the moonlight.

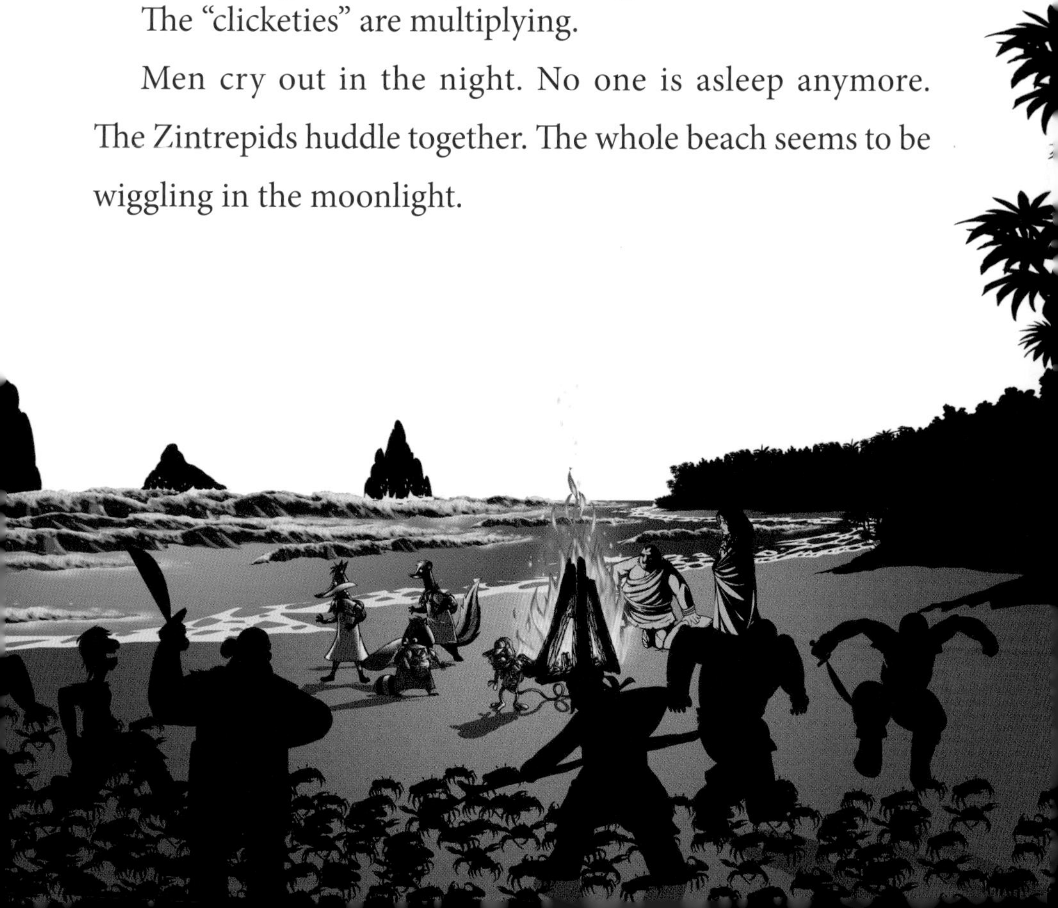

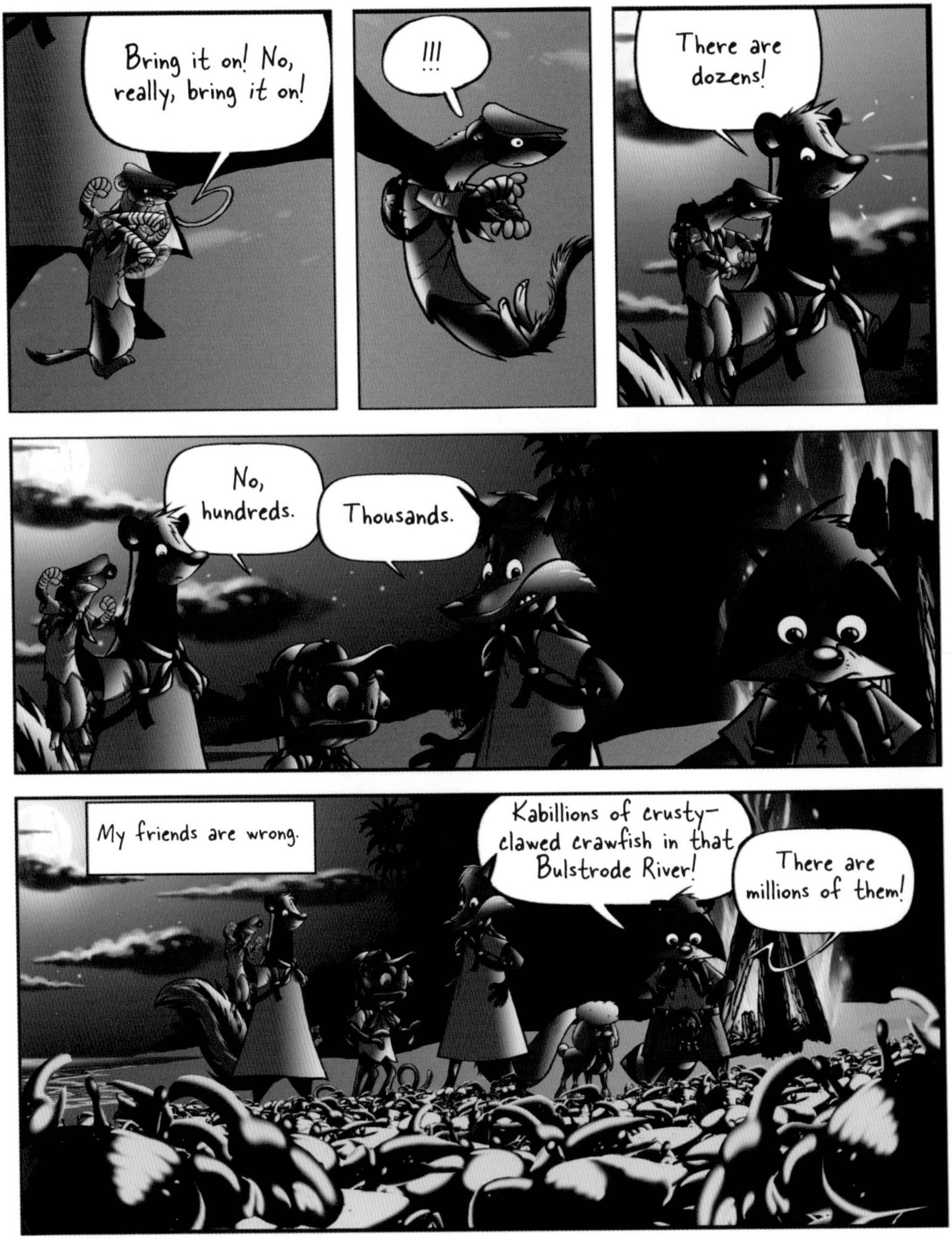
Bring it on! No, really, bring it on!
!!!
...
There are dozens!
No, hundreds.
Thousands.
My friends are wrong.
Kabillions of crusty-clawed crawfish in that Bulstrode River!
There are millions of them!

Chapter 16

The Sideways Menace

Under the cover of darkness, the crabs have crawled out from their hiding spots in the sand, in pursuit of food.

And in this case, that's us!

The crabs are everywhere, as far as the eye can see.

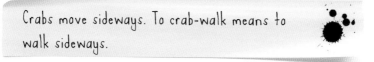

Crabs move sideways. To crab-walk means to walk sideways.

We are practically surrounded. The *ONLY EXIT* possible is the SEA. We can't take refuge on our boat, as it is sitting roughly thirty meters out in the water, nor in the jungle, because the crustaceans are blocking our way to it.

We join the crew to confront this new menace together, as a united front.

Each sailor holds out a TORCH to fend off this swarm of crabs, keeping them at bay. Otherwise we'd be cooked. FrouFrou barks incessantly, which, unlike with the sirens, has no effect on the crabs. When this doesn't work, he launchs himself toward me so I can protect him.

"Don't even think about it!" I tell him, panicking.

"Really, Billy Stuart!" Foxy scolds. "Come to see me, my darling FrouFrou. I'll protect you!"

The poodle wags his tail at the sound of his friend's voice and takes refuge in her arms.

CLICKETY CLICKETY

The sound of the shells colliding is unnerving. I think I prefer the sirens' call to this.

With the fire from her torch, Timoree burns the approaching first line, and the delicious smell of roasting crabs starts to waft.

YUM! YUM!

Quick as lightning, I seize a cooked crab and sink my teeth into it.

CRUNCH! CRUNCH! CRUNCH!

"It's crunchilicious!" Nowhere near as delicious as those Bulstrode river crawfish, but not bad at all.

Shifty, with his long tongue, grabs a tiny cooked crab.

CRUNCH! CRUNCH! CRUNCH!

"Yummy," he says. "That's very edible. And it's better than scorpion, with that tail…"

Our feast is rather ironic, given that in only a few minutes we will be on the crabs' menu. It's a bit like a condemned person's last meal.

CLICKETY CLICKETY

Overcome by the sheer number of little critters, we are likely going to be descaled, devoured, digested and returned to the earth.

Soon the **FLAMES** of our torches start to die down. We can't keep them going for much longer. But the crabs keep advancing, practically against their will, pushed forward by the imposing mass behind them.

CLICKETY CLICKETY

I wonder how it will happen. Will they start with my tail, or my delicate fingers? Not my nose, I hope! This thought upsets me so much that I'm almost in tears!

"What a waste," I say to Foxy, who is standing beside me.

"A waste, Billy Stuart?" she repeats.

"Yes, a waste! I can't believe it. Dying like this, after all we've been through, after having braved thousands of dangers at sea."

Remember the title of the book...

The fox doesn't quite know how to respond.

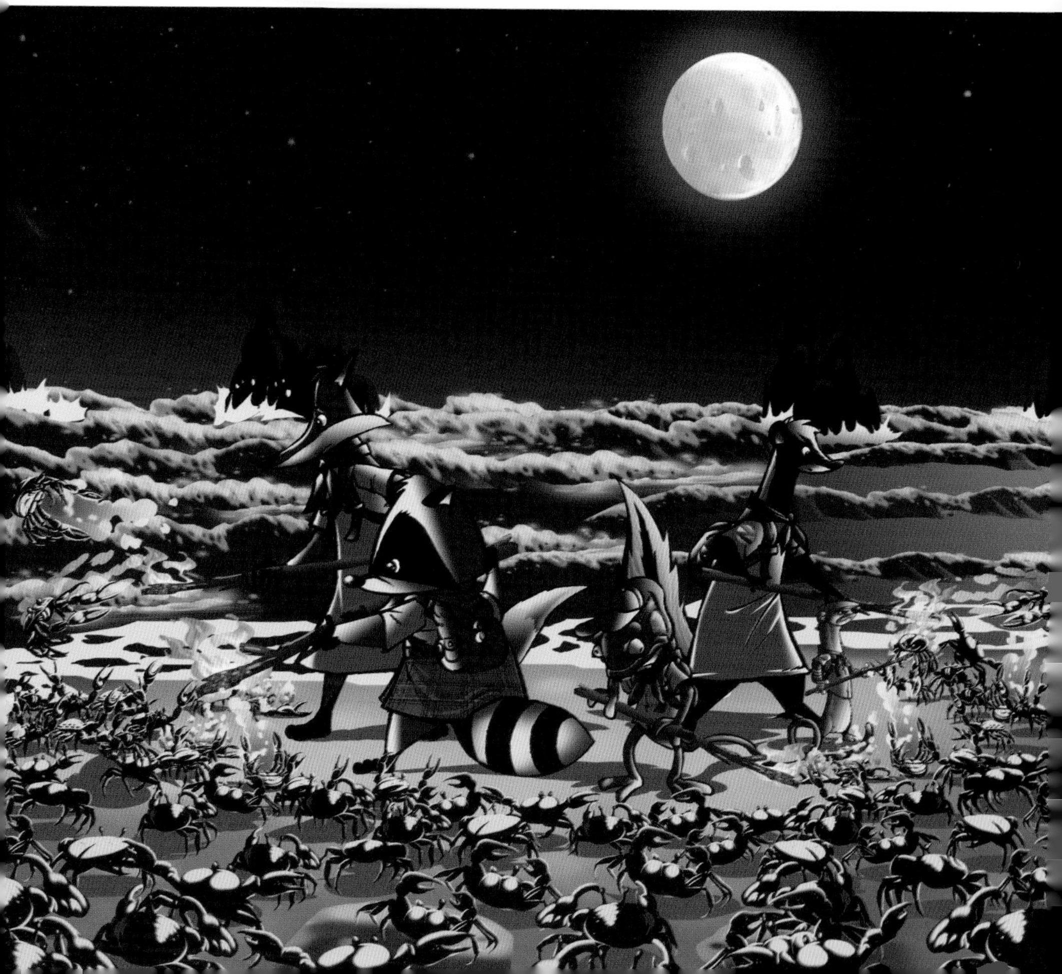

Even Yeti, who's normally the first one to take on a new adversary, stays quiet. The crabs are getting closer and closer. **I AM TERRIFIED**.

Then suddenly the CLICKETY CLICKS stop.

Above our heads a gigantic black silhouette obscures the moon. The creepy crabs all stop moving. A bloodcurdling scream erupts above us.

AAAAAAAAAAAARK!

The roc!

We're on his island!

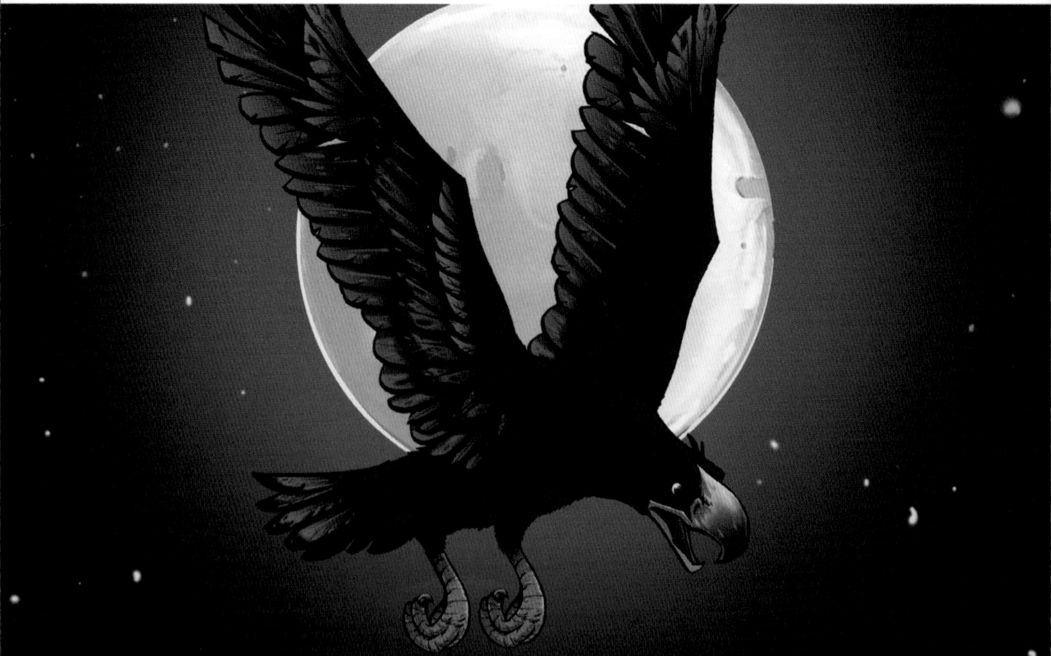

The Winged Ally

"This is the last straw!" Musky sighs, incredulous at seeing the massive bird again. "Seriously?!? I bet the sirens are watching all this from the sea with that squid."

I correct her. "The octopus."

"Humph," she replies.

And here we go again. Squid, octopus...whatever!

AAAAAAAARK!

The roc brings us back to the moment. It lands on the beach, directly on the crab carpet. With his landing comes the **DISGUSTING** sound of shells being crushed.

CRAAAAAAAAACK!

Which rhymes with the roc's cry:

AAAAAAAAAAAARK!

As for us, we think it's gross and cry:

"**YUCK!**"

Is the bird going to attack us?

Apparently not. In one beak-load he gets dozens of crabs, which he then crunches on. This sows the seed of panic among the crustaceans. Great! As long as they don't all head in our direction!

The crabs sidestep back to their shelters in the sand and bury themselves quickly, hundreds at a time.

AAAAAAARK!

The beast isn't finished. Resting on the beach, he beats his wings powerfully, tossing thousands of crabs into the sea.

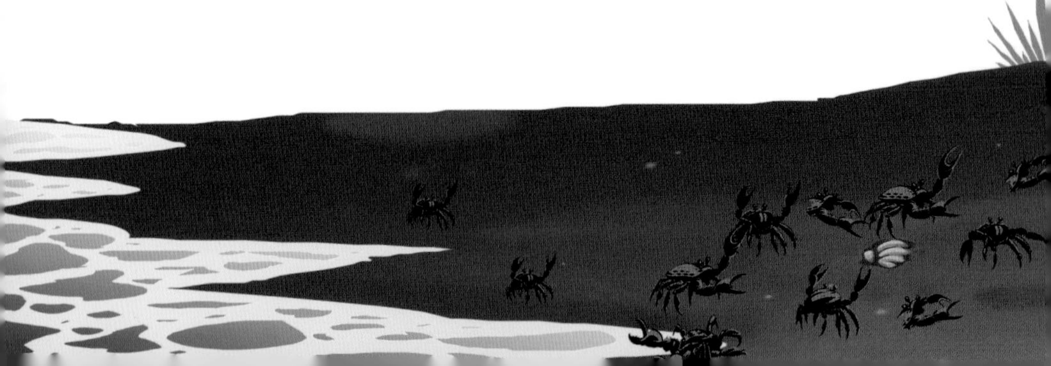

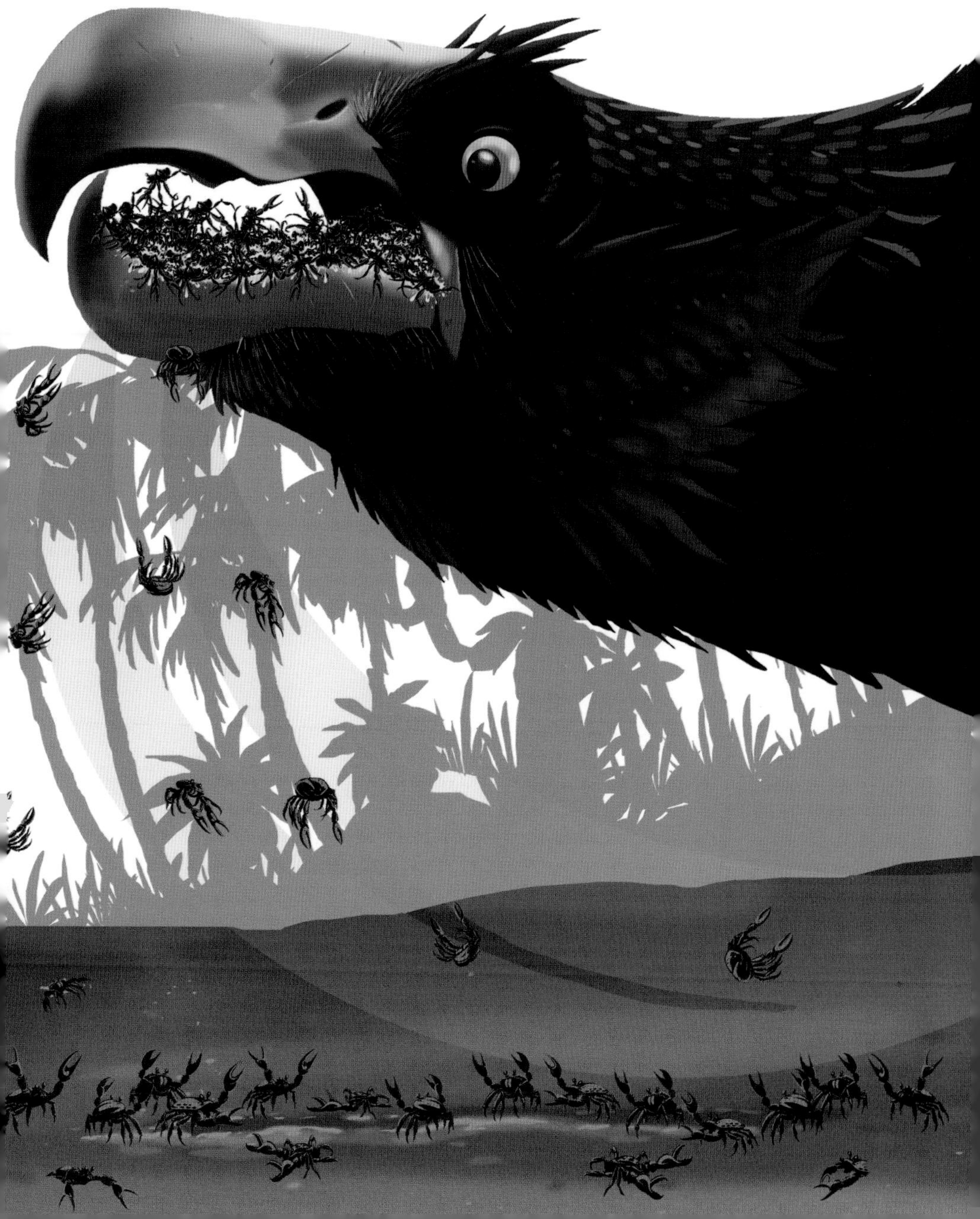

The monster wipes the beach clean.

All that's left is us.

The bird turns his head to see us better. The moonlight and the dying fire provide enough light for him to see us. As if he recognizes someone, he walks toward…Foxy!

"I can SPRAY him if you want, Foxy," the skunk suggests quietly.

"That won't be necessary, Musky," the fox replies calmly.

Without any fear, she watches the giant WINGED CREATURE move toward her. FrouFrou, in Foxy's arms, barks at the beast's approach.

A few meters from the fox, the roc stops. With one strike of his beak he could devour her. The sailors are ready to jump into action, brandishing their weapons and their flickering TORCHES.

I clear my throat and say to Foxy:

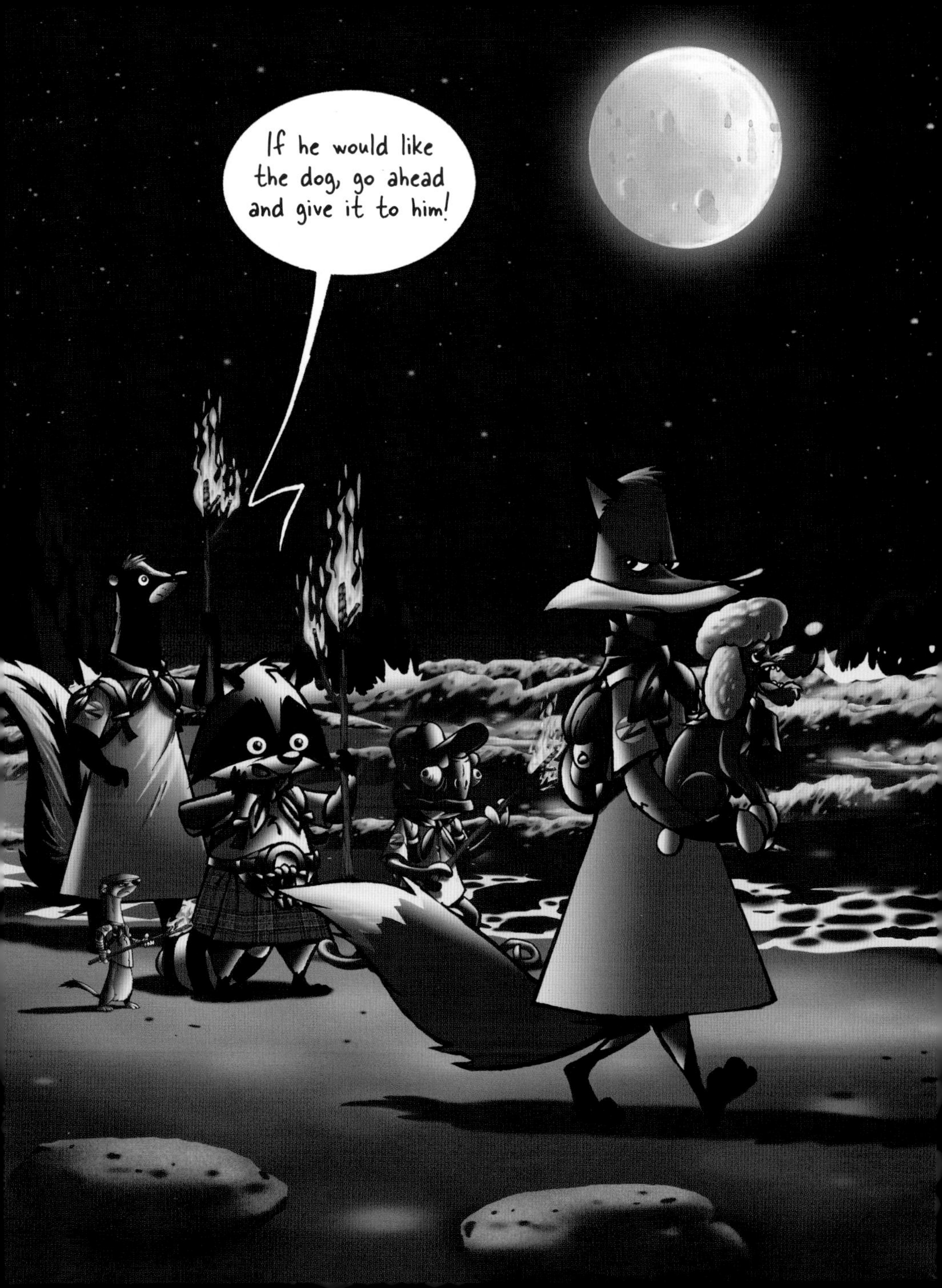
If he would like the dog, go ahead and give it to him!

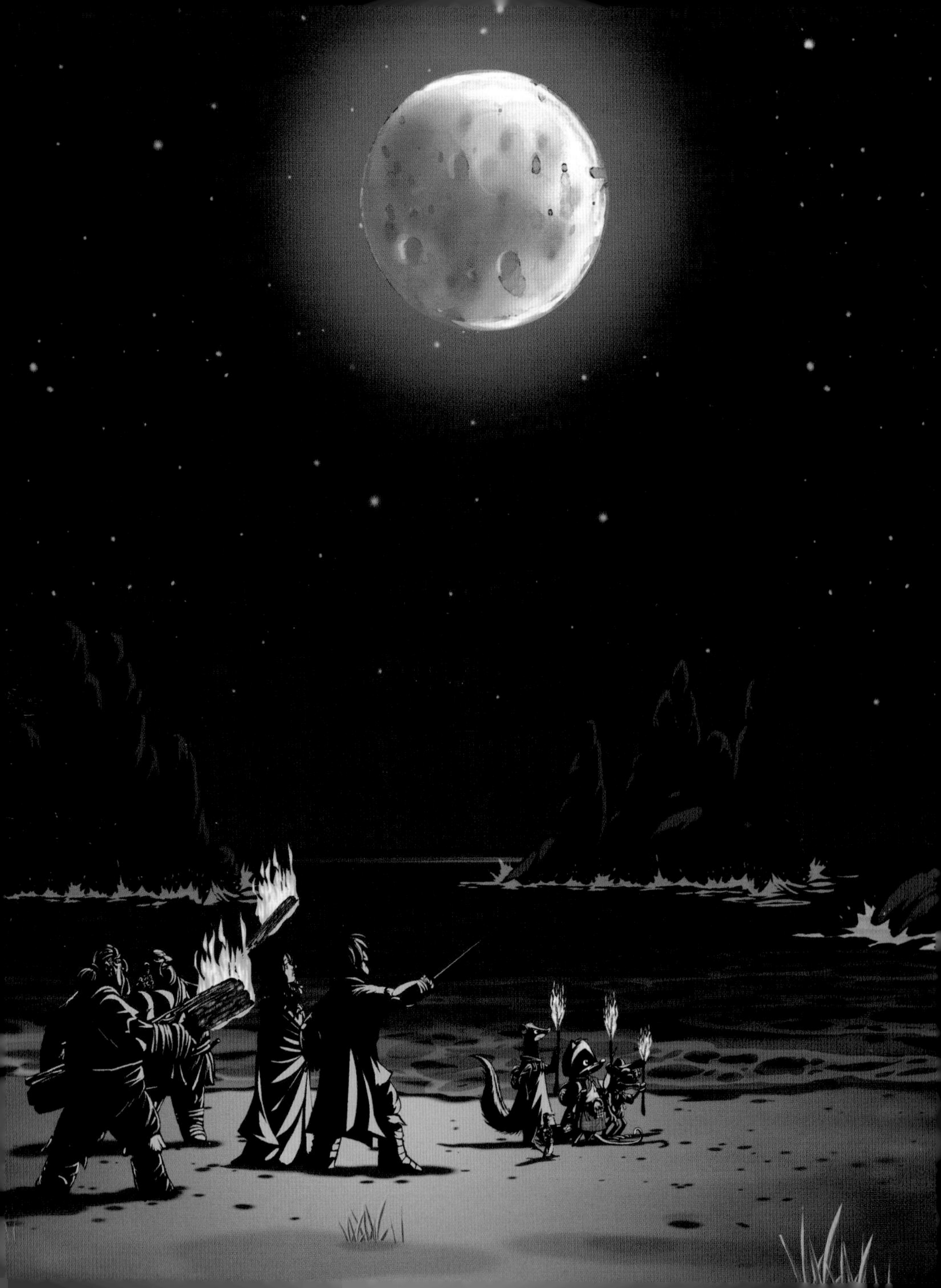

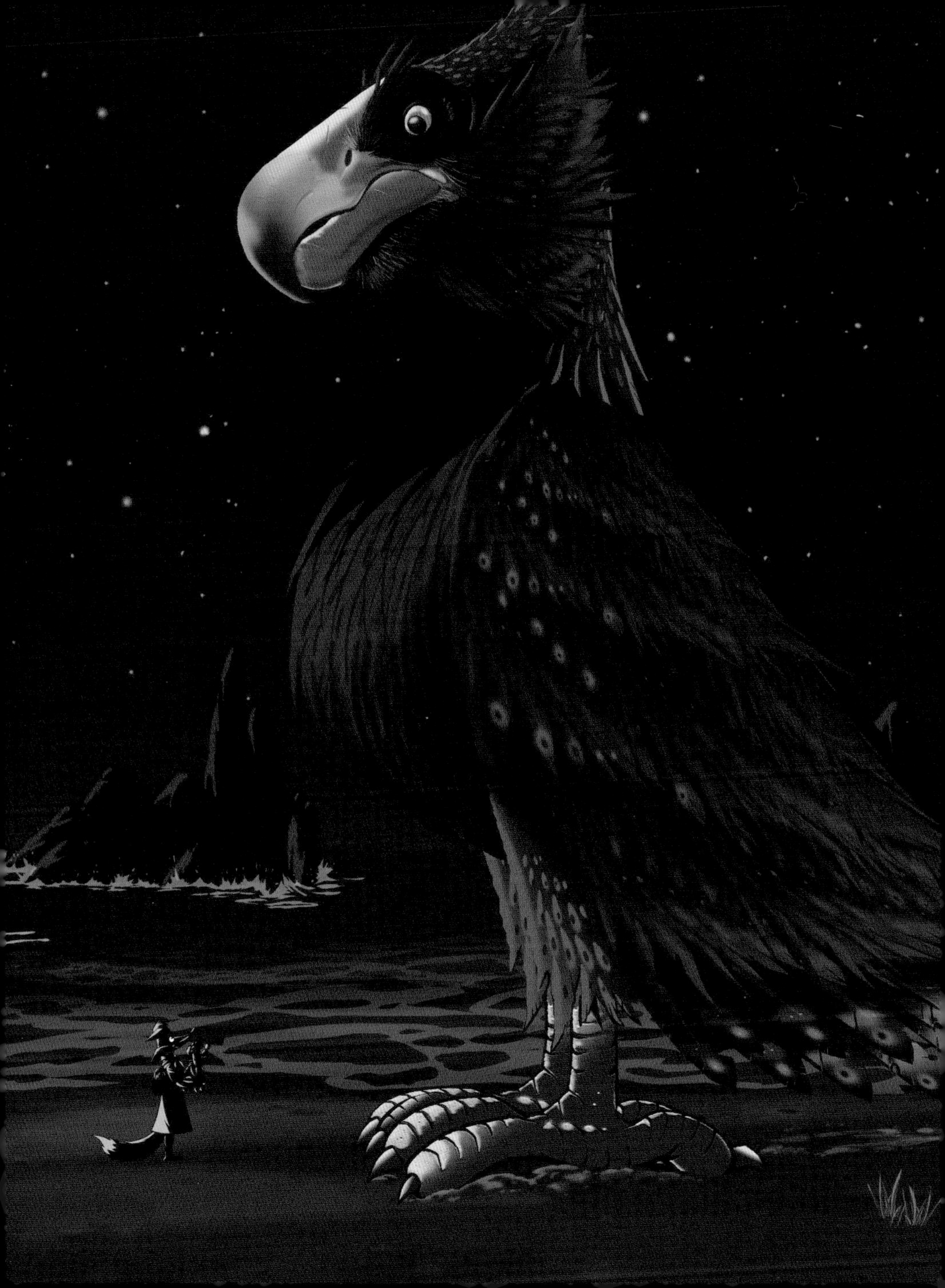

The roc bows majestically before Foxy, accepting a cuddle. The fox scratches the roc's giant **NECK** with a mixture of respect and fascination.

"I think he's thanking her for helping him in his fight with the octopus," Shifty says.

The bird cocks his head suddenly, listening, then takes off with *GRACE* and **VIGOR**, lifting a cloud of sand beneath him.

"It's like someone just called him," says a surprised Foxy.

The brilliant moonlight allows us to see our winged ally as he glides over the JUNGLE and then vanishes into the darkness, back to wherever he came from. He lets out a last cry, a goodbye, as he flies away.

AAAAAAAAAARK!

Silence falls. Losloblos asks three of the men to go look for more wood to relight the fire.

"Crabs there!" shouts Shifty.

Now that the roc has disappeared, they've come out of their hiding places.

AAAAAAAAAAAAARKKK!

The crabs, scared again, retreat back under the sand.

Impressed, I congratulate Timoree.

"Great imitation!"

For the rest of the NIGHT, the crabs stay hidden in their shelter.

The crab attack reminds me of a story I read a long time ago, *The Undersea Menace*, by Henri Vernes. The cover's illustration was gripping. You could see Bob Morane and his friend, Bill Ballantine, buried up to their shoulders in the sand on a beach. Coming toward them were hundreds of crabs. In devouring the book, I learned that our heroes pulled off a remarkable escape before they became the crabs' dinner. "Yes," said Billy Stuart when I told him the anecdote, "except the story of Bob Morane happened in a book. This is *real life*." What more can I say?

Grandfather Virgil's Notebook

This time, it's a different kind of cry that wakes us from our sandy bed.

AAAAAAAAAARK!

Curiously, this one sounds like a rooster.

I wake up the Zintrepids. The poodle dances on his hind legs, *excited* by the prospect of a new day on a seemingly deserted island.

We join the crew for our first meal since the shipwreck (bananas and coconuts, no eggs or bacon or FROOT LOOPS).

Half asleep, Foxy asks, "Where are the toilets?"

I point toward the sea on one side and the jungle on the other.

"Your choice."

The fox yawns and stretches.

"Why do we have to get up at ℝOOSTER O'CLOCK? We're on holidays," she complains, puffing out her tail.

Rooster o'clock means pretty early in the morning, thank you very much.

"Wait till I get my hands on that RooSTER!" says Musky.

I tell them the rooster is actually one of the sailors who's been keeping watch. He pretended to be the roc to discourage the crabs from another outing.

Loslobos gathers everyone together.

"We are going to explore the island. I'll need a dozen men. The others will stay near the ship."

Volunteers step forward. I consult the Zintrepids.

"I don't want to just sit around, Billy Stuart," says Shifty. "Let's move!"

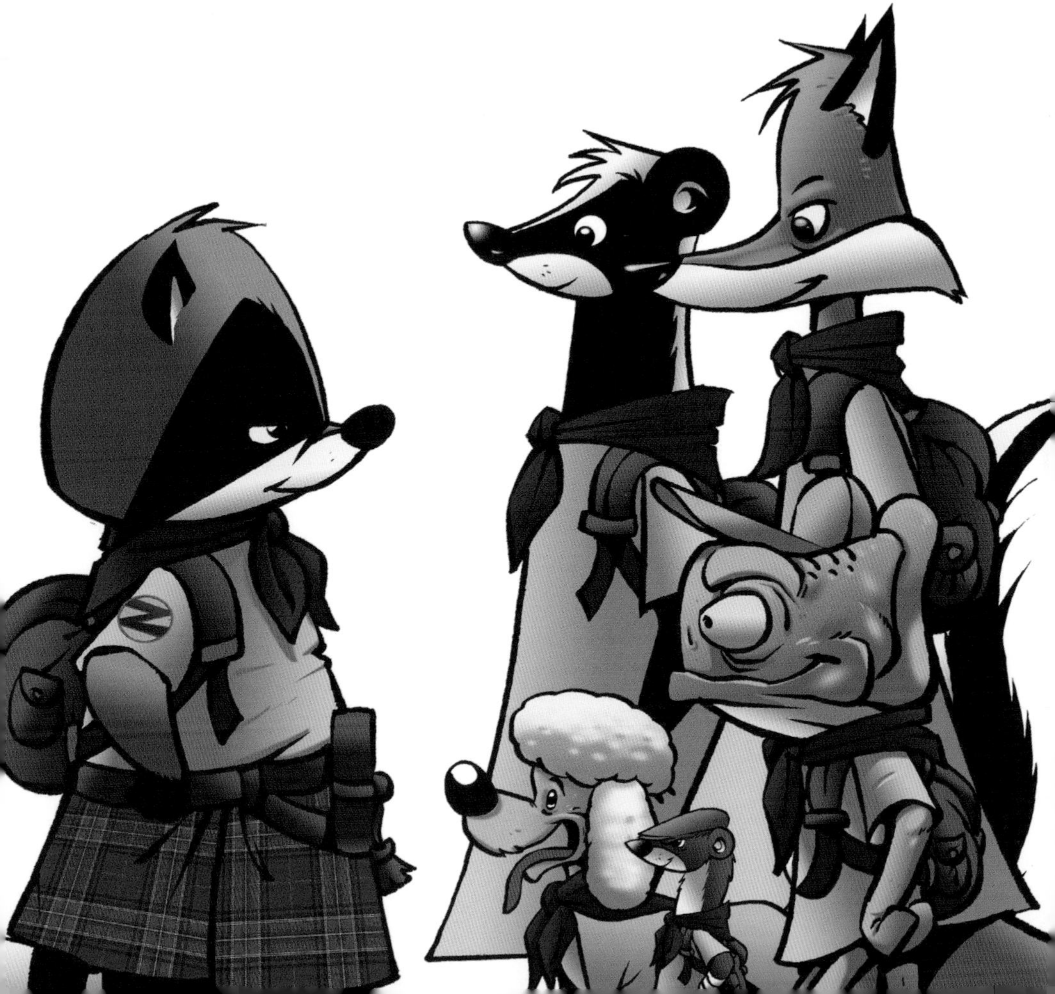

And so here we are, trying to move through a path in the jungle, in horrendous heat.

Everyone is on the lookout for wild animals, but we never hear any telltale **CRIES** or **NOISES**. The animals are either very private, or they aren't there. I prefer the second hypothesis.

As we progress, our surroundings barely change—just dense jungle with strange trees with large **TRUNKS**, broad leaves and ropey vines all over them. Anyone with some imagination could have mistaken them for snakes…

Only Tarzan, the human monkey, was missing. No relation to my hairy brother-in-law.

Here and there, unusual flowers with **SPECTACULAR COLORS** grow. Giant insects, almost like dragonflies but some as big as my hand, are flying among the flowers. Their buzzing troubles me a bit.

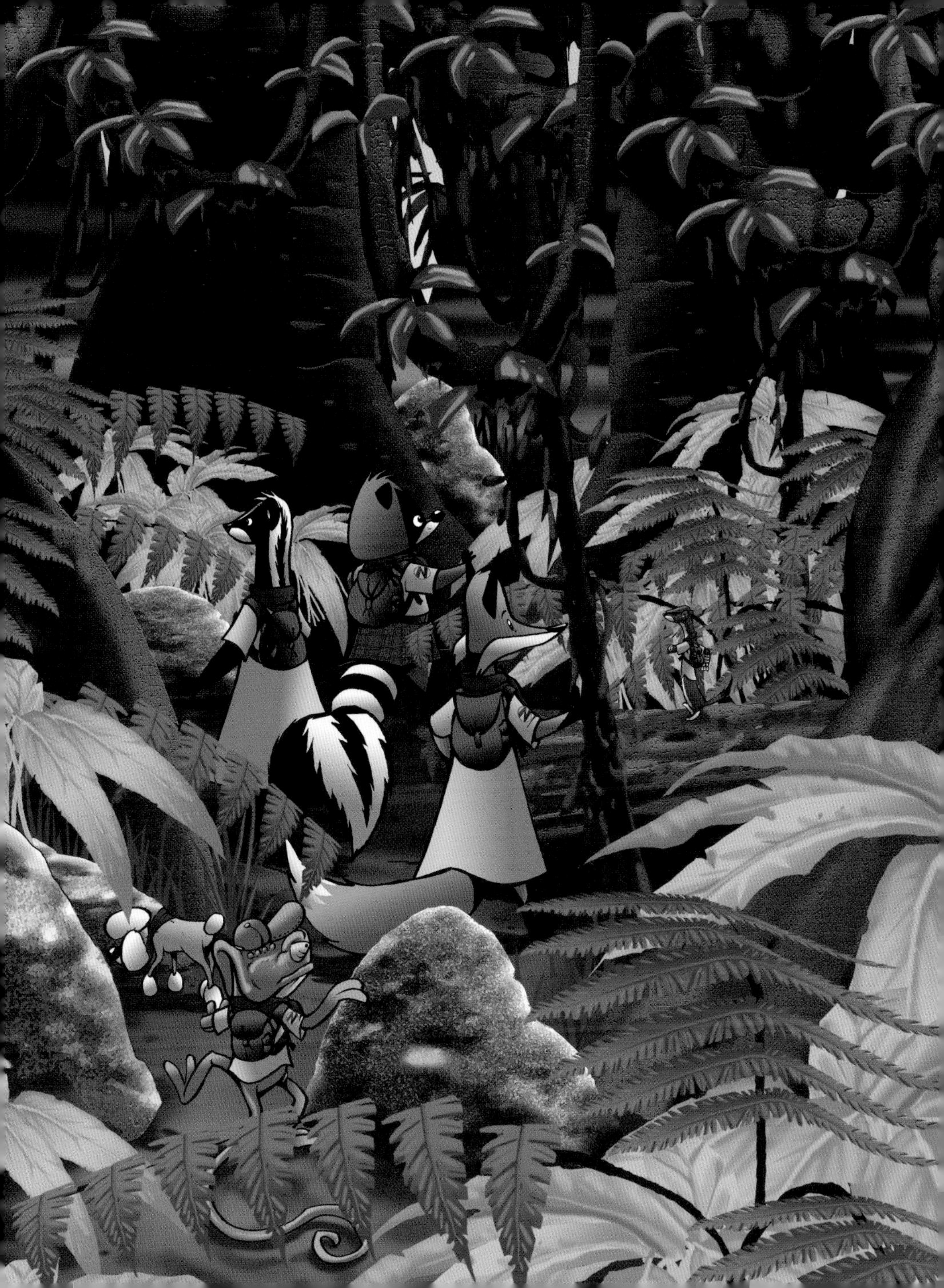

After an hour of walking, the captain calls for a break.

I sit down on the trunk of a fallen tree.

"You're quiet, Billy Stuart," says Foxy, sitting down near me. "What's worrying you?"

I pull out my grandfather Virgil's NOTEBOOK from my purse. Distractedly I flip through it. After the first few pages, there is no more writing. We are totally in the dark.

"You see, Foxy, I don't know where we're going. I don't know if we're still following my grandfather's footsteps."

BZZZZZZZZZZZZZ

A massive insect buzzes above our heads. Foxy is petrified, and I don't dare move—I don't want to irritate it.

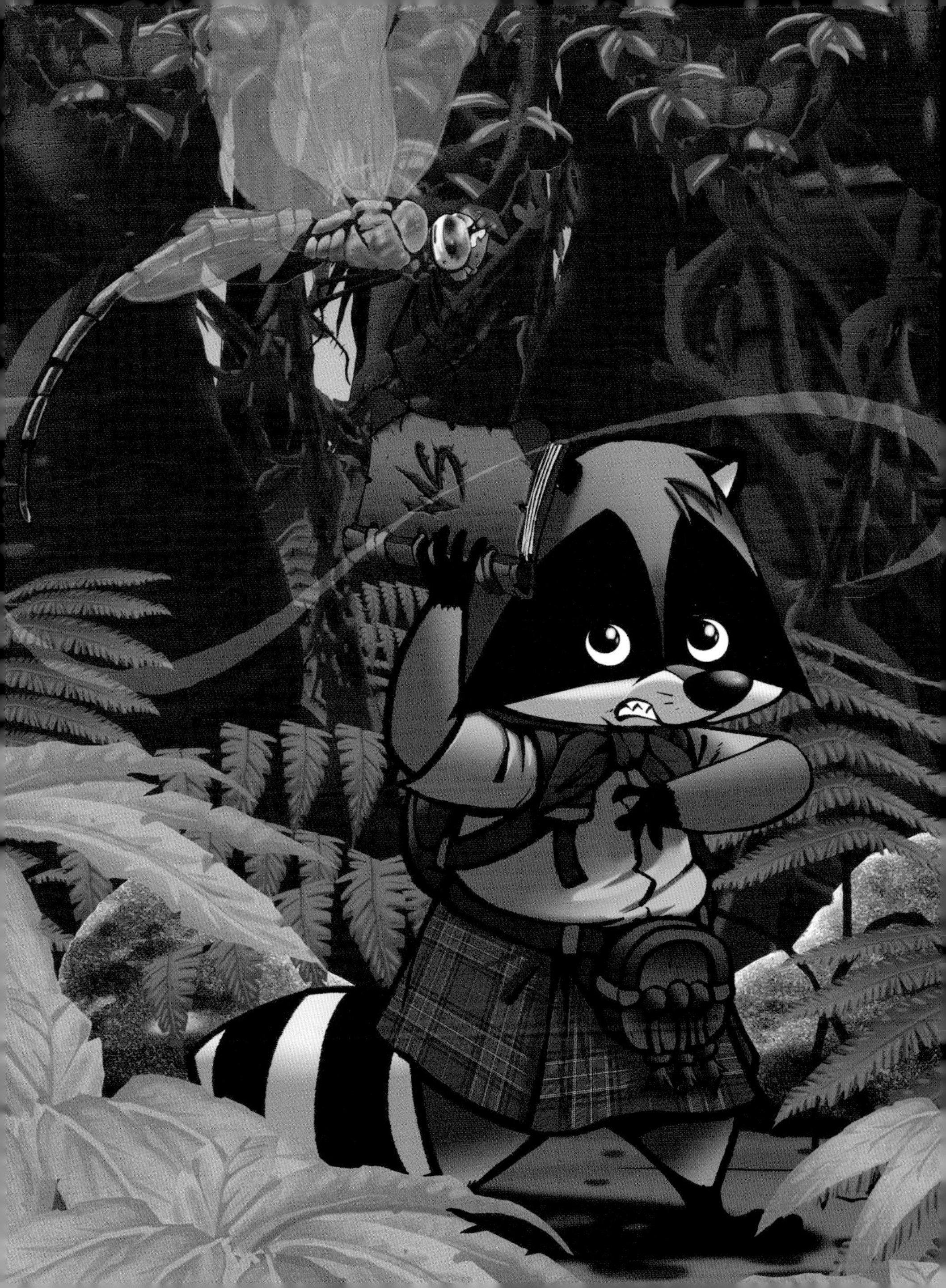

The enormous beast lands right on my snout! I squint. I think it's a dragonfly, but I don't know what kind.

Yeti approaches with his fists clenched.

"Do you want me to **CRUSH** it? On your **NOSE?**"

"Nope," I say, whispering as if I am worried the insect might hear me.

"It's just a big dragonfly," says Musky. "I could SPRAY, Billy Stuart, if you want. If you close your mouth?"

"No!" I wave him away.

Shifty examines the insect. He is practically salivating.

"I could just eat it, Billy Stuart," he suggests.

"No again, no and no!" The dragonfly is tightly gripping my snout. If the chameleon's tongue were to touch it, or if Shifty sprayed, I would have a serious problem!

Then, no doubt getting bored, the insect takes off, flies all around my head, tickling my ears, then lands delicately on the pages of the notebook.

This is my chance!

I quickly close the notebook.

SNAP!

SQUISH!

"**YUUUUUUUCK!**" the Zintrepids say in unison.

A drop of GREEN LIQUID runs down the skinny little green leg sticking out of the notebook. The dragonfly wiggles a bit more. Then nothing.

Carefully I open the notebook. The dragonfly serves as a bookmark. It's squashed and spread across the two pages.

I gag.

Foxy rips a large leaf from a tree and gives it to me to wipe off the mess. Holding the notebook as far away from me as possible, I try to chase away the stain.

An exercise in pronunciation. Repeat with Billy Stuart:
I chase the tenacious stain with tenacity.

"**OOOOOOOH!**" exclaim the Zintrepids.

KABILLIONS of crusty-clawed crawfish in that Bulstrode River!

The GREEN LIQUID reveals yet another secret contained in the notebook.

The right-hand side page shows a drawing of an immense eyeball with a handwritten entry. And it is my grandfather Virgil's HANDWRITING!

Be careful, Billy Stuart. Someone on the island is keeping an eye on you...

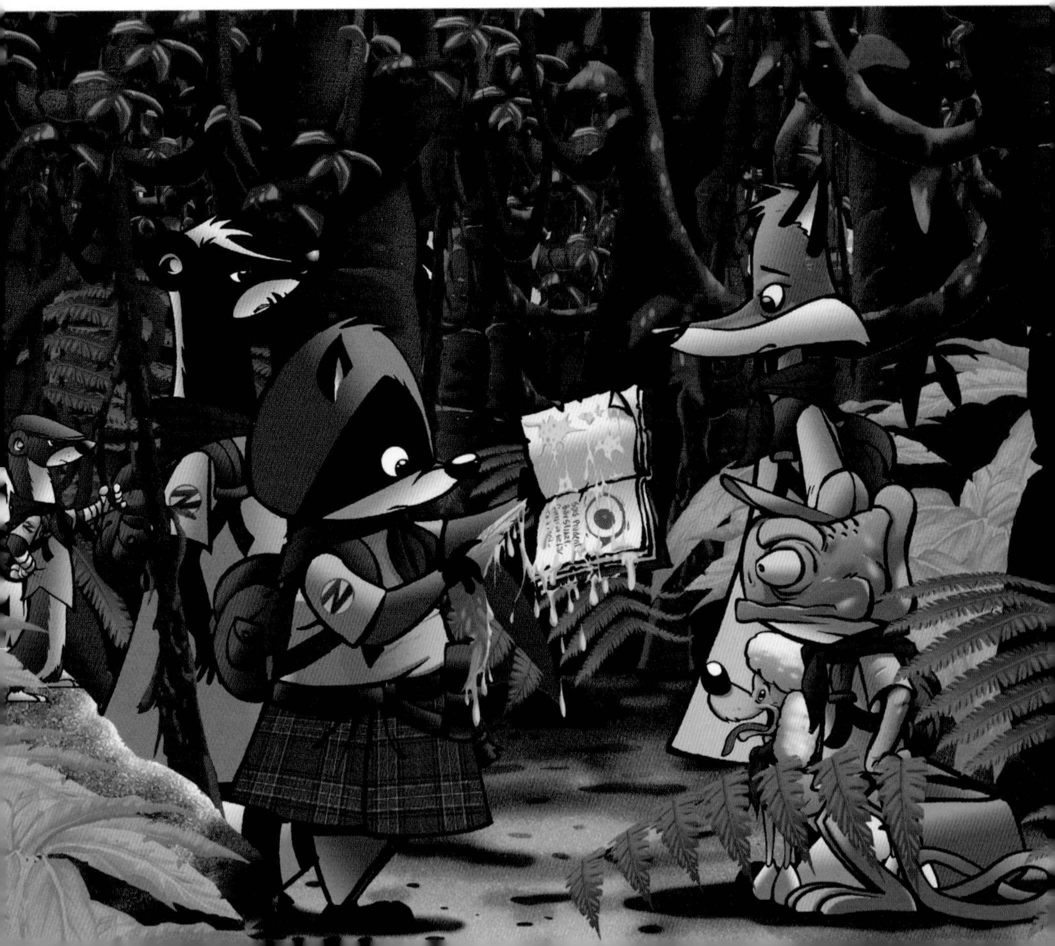

Grant me one last favor, dear reader. The title of this book deserves an explanation. As perceptive as you are, you'll have noticed that the dangers don't add up to a thousand.

If you have been keeping track, you'll remember the storm, the major calm afterward when the wind died, the mutiny of the crew, the "attacks" from the roc, the octopus and the sirens. (What about the crabs, you say? They were on the beach in the sand, not in the sea.) So we are up to six dangers in all. On the other hand, Billy Stuart swears that someone estimated there to be at least 995 sirens.

So to recap: 995 sirens + the storm + the absence of wind for several days + the mutiny + the roc + the octopus = 1,000 dangers.

Hence the title: *The Sea of a Thousand Dangers.*

We can all agree that the title works for the book?

As Billy Stuart would say, "Kabillions of crusty-clawed crawfish in that Bulstrode River!"

And here we can write the words **THE END.**

SEARCH AND FIND

Can you spot these items in the book?

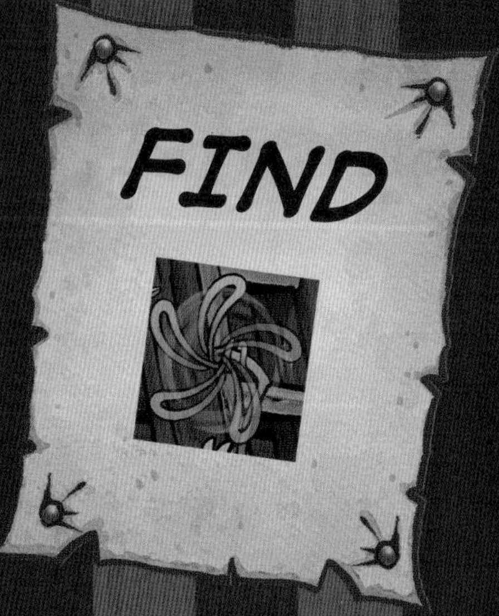
FIND

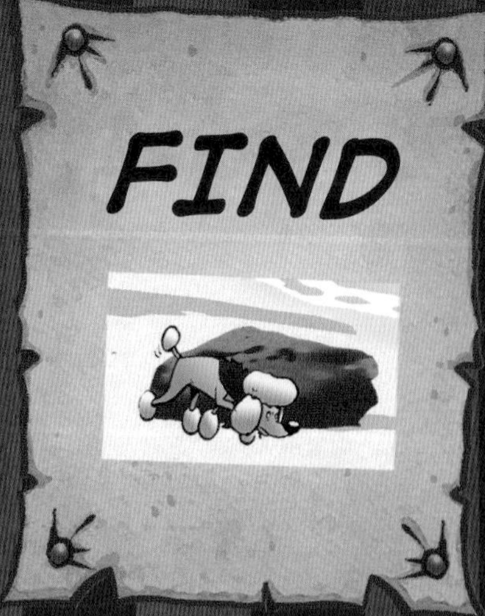
FIND

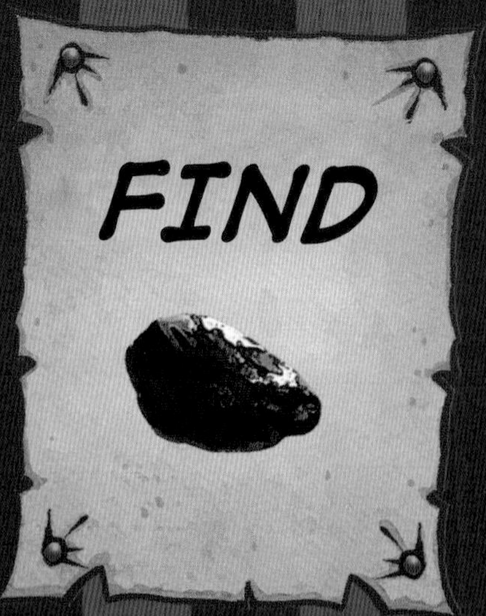
FIND

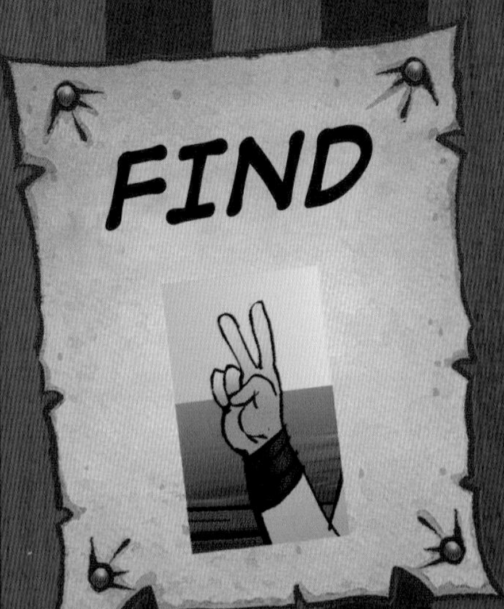
FIND

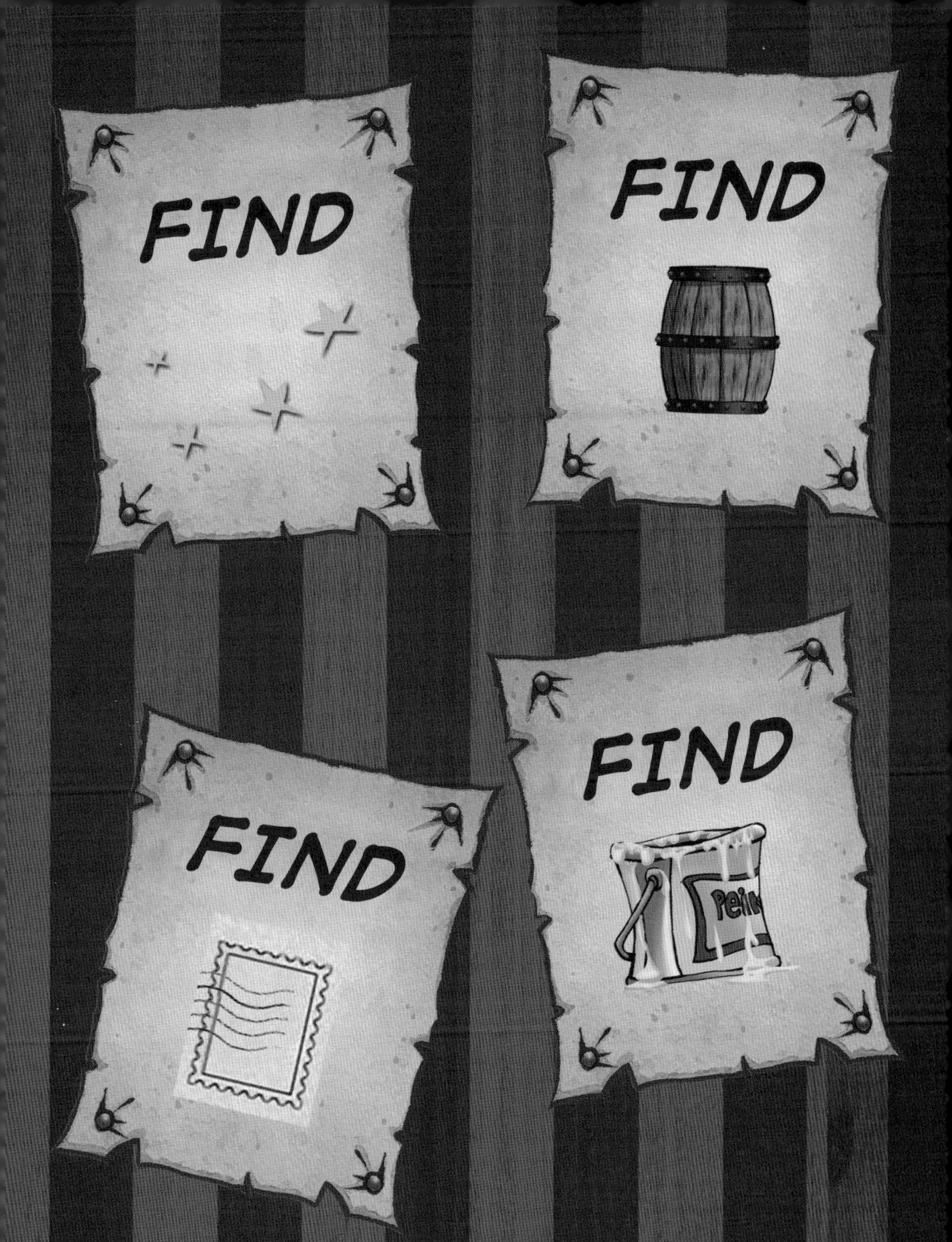
FIND
FIND
FIND
FIND
Pein

Solution on page 143.

SOLUTIONS

FUNNY FACES! (P. 16)

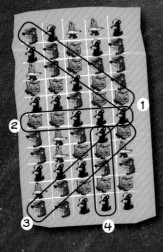

THE SHOPKEEPER'S CHALLENGE (P. 22)

FIRST BILLY WILL WEIGH TWO GROUPS OF THREE CRAWFISH, ONE GROUP ON EACH SCALE PAN. IF A PAN LEANS TO ONE SIDE, IT MEANS THE HEAVIEST CRAWFISH IS ON THAT SCALE. IF THEY BALANCE, IT MEANS THE CRAWFISH WEIGH THE SAME, SO THE HEAVIEST CRAWFISH IS IN THE THIRD GROUP.

WHEN HE HAS DETERMINED THE GROUP WITH THE HEAVIEST CRAWFISH, BILLY PLACES ONE CRAWFISH FROM THE THIRD GROUP ON EACH SCALE PAN. HE WILL BE ABLE TO DETERMINE EASILY IF THE CRAWFISH HE IS LOOKING FOR IS ON THE SCALE OR IF IT'S THE ONE REMAINING.